"Mama doesn't think Beau would make a good husband for me."

Calvin pulled her closer to him, till his eyes were only inches from her own. "Neither do I," he said. "I—oh, Sarah. Could I—? Do you mind if I kiss you?"

Her heart was pounding in her chest and her knees were weak as wilted greens, but she knew what she wanted.

"I don't mind," she whispered. "I think I would like—"

He didn't wait for any more words, but bent and kissed her. And it was wonderful, so much better than Beau's kisses that she could hardly believe it. When Beau kissed her, even on the cheek, she wanted to run off and wash her cheek, scrub it hard. But when Calvin kissed her, she wanted never to wash that place again.

She wanted to hold it forever in her heart—her first kiss from Calvin.

NINA COOMBS PYKARE has been writing novels for over twenty years. Recently widowed, Nina is a native resident of northeastern Ohio, and she has five grown children and several grandchildren.

Books by Nina Coombs Pykare

HEARTSONG PRESENTS
HP190—A Matter of Faith

Neither Bond Nor Free

Nina Coombs Pykare

Heartsong Presents

A note from the author:
*I love to hear from my readers! You may correspond with me
by writing:* **Nina Coombs Pykare
Author Relations
PO Box 719
Uhrichsville, OH 44683**

ISBN 1-57748-937-3

NEITHER BOND NOR FREE

Scripture quotations marked KJV are taken from the King James
Version of the Bible.

All of the characters and events in this book are fictitious. Any
resemblance to actual persons, living or dead, or to actual events
is purely coincidental.

Cover illustration by Lauraine Bush.

PRINTED IN THE U.S.A.

one

Richmond, Virginia—October 1859

"One hundred," the burly auctioneer said. The small black boy on the auction block stared straight in front of him, his face stolid, his eyes unseeing. His hands hung limply at his sides. The ragged homespun shirt that covered him stopped just above his knees, leaving his legs and feet bare, scabbed beneath the dried mud that streaked them.

In the front row of the crowd, Calvin Sharp shifted from one booted foot to the other and scanned the faces around him. Josiah Cooper wasn't in this room. Calvin swallowed a sigh. He ought to get out of this place, but something kept him there, standing, watching. He swallowed hard and kept his face from revealing his disgust. He'd known slavery existed, of course, but this was his first trip to the South. He'd never come face-to-face with the reality before, never actually seen a little child auctioned off like—like an animal.

It was one thing to make an occasional contribution to the Anti-Slavery League. He'd done that as a matter of course, as any man raised by his mother would. He'd also heard about some kind of underground system, the Underground Railroad, it was called, that moved runaway slaves north to Canada. And he'd sympathized with its work—in the abstract.

But this—the selling of children—the horror of this ripped at a man's guts, made him want to lose his latest meal or start tearing the place to pieces. He did neither, of course. A Pinkerton operative had to be in control of himself. At all times.

"He's just a little 'un now," the auctioneer told the crowd, raising the boy's scrawny arm and releasing it to drop limply to his side. "But he'll grow. You'll see, in a year or so, he'll pick lotsa cotton."

The boy's teeth were clamped on his lower lip, and he didn't utter a sound. A brave child—or too scared to cry. Calvin couldn't be sure which.

"Two hundred," the auctioneer said, nodding to a rather slovenly planter who stood halfway round the circle, a cheroot dangling from his fat jowls.

To his left, Calvin heard a muffled sob. The boy's mother perhaps. He turned. But the sob had come from a white woman—a girl actually. Tears stood in her huge violet eyes, and her pale hands twisted a handkerchief that she'd wrung almost to pieces.

The slave girl beside her, roughly the same age, looked too young to be the child's mother, even though the planters bred slaves young. But from the granite set of her mouth, she was related to him and trying hard not to break down.

The boy ventured a quick look at the bidder, then looked away even quicker, fear in his dark eyes. The fat man was evidently well-known—and not for a kind heart. The little fellow's bare knees were beginning to quiver.

"Do I hear three hundred?" the auctioneer asked.

Calvin felt the bile rising in his throat. His boyhood hadn't been easy, but the worst of Chicago's slums had been better than this! At least there everyone was considered human. No one ever assumed another was a thing—to be bought and sold, like a pig or a cow.

"Going, going—"

"Three hundred," Calvin heard himself say. What was he doing? Had he lost his mind? Three hundred was almost all he'd saved in his years as a Pinkerton operative. And it was just about all he had with him for expenses.

Besides, he didn't need a slave. He didn't *want* a slave. The whole idea of owning another human being was abhorrent to him. He squared his shoulders. Well, God had obviously put the words in his mouth. So it seemed he was under orders not to let that fat brute carry off the child. He'd just have to wire Chicago for more funds. It was common knowledge at home that the chief was against slavery. Surely he'd understand this.

The fat planter gave Calvin an appraising glance, his beady eyes squinting in unuttered menace. But Calvin met his gaze serenely. It took more than a hard stare to cow a Pinkerton man. The planter looked away first, then he shuffled forward and prodded the boy in the ribs. The boy took it, staring stolidly into the distance. Finally the planter shook his head and muttered, "Nope. Not worth it."

The room grew quiet. Calvin held his breath and breathed a silent prayer. *Please, Lord, if You want me to take this boy away from here, don't let anyone else bid on him.*

Finally the auctioneer said, "Sold." Calvin released his breath slowly and tried to look as if he bought slaves every day. Then, still wondering how he'd gotten himself into this predicament, he went forward to pay out the money and receive the papers that said he now owned one small black boy who looked at him from fearful eyes.

Calvin lifted him down, nothing but skin and bones really, and led him away from the block and its terrors. Near the wall Calvin hunkered down, bringing his eyes level with the boy's. "What's your name, boy?"

The boy's eyes were big. "Willie, Massa."

"Well, Willie, you won't be picking any cotton."

Willie nodded, his somber face indicating he expected a fate even worse than picking cotton. "What I gonna do then, Massa?"

That was the question. What *could* the boy do?

"You'll just travel around with me, I guess. Run errands, maybe. That kind of thing." He put a hand on the boy's slight shoulder. "Maybe keep me company. You think you can do that?"

Willie's smile was blinding. "Yes, Massa. I do that good! I be the bestest boy you ever had."

"Good." Calvin straightened. Now he had to get out of this place, had to be about the work the chief had sent him here to do. He'd traced the counterfeiter Josiah Cooper as far as Richmond, and then he'd lost him. But he was a Pinkerton man and he would—

"Excuse me, sir." The low melodious tones came from behind him, from a female throat.

He turned. The young woman who stood there was smiling now, not crying. A planter's daughter, he guessed. Her fashionable bonnet and shawl showed she was well-off. And up close she was even more beautiful than he'd thought.

"Calvin," he said, managing to make his unruly tongue work at last. "The name's Calvin Sharp." She was so beautiful, her eyes still lustrous with tears. Under the bonnet her dark hair framed a peaches-and-cream complexion. And the sprigged dimity gown shaped a figure just reaching womanhood.

The slave girl fell to her knees and took the boy in her arms.

"I done a'right, Minta?" he asked.

"You done real good, Willie, real good."

"Thank you, sir," the young white woman said, smiling up into Calvin's face. "We were afraid, so afraid—"

She looked like such a delicate creature. How could she be part of this evil? "Did the boy belong to you?" he asked.

"To my father," she said, anguish in her voice. "My father, Colonel Hawthorne. I tried. I begged him not to sell Willie." She gestured toward the slave girl. "He's Minta's brother. All that's left of her family." She swallowed. "I begged. But Papa said sentiment has no place in running a business."

A business! A business in human bodies. Calvin bit back the angry words that rose in his throat. There was no use in raging at the girl. She was obviously in distress. And what could a mere girl do anyway?

"Is your father here today?" he inquired, glancing around.

She shuddered delicately. "Oh, no. Papa leaves the selling to the overseer, Vickers. That's him over there, in the vermilion waistcoat."

Calvin looked. This Vickers was a disreputable specimen if he'd ever seen one—his coat, trousers, and boots spattered with mud, and his body, what could be seen of it, not much cleaner. The vermilion waistcoat was starting to fray, his wide-brimmed planter's hat rested on greasy hanks of hair, and his eyes gleamed with the evil that Calvin had already met, the evil that knew no regard for human life.

The girl shuddered again. "Don't let him catch you watching him. He might—he might tell Papa."

Moved by her distress, Calvin turned back to her.

"The boy will be all right. I promise. If you'll tell me your name and where to reach you, I'll even let you know how he's doing."

"Jesus bless you, Massa," the slave girl whispered, gratitude shining in her eyes.

"Yes, the Lord bless you," the young woman said, her lips curving in a smile. "We'd like to hear about Willie. You may address a letter to me—Sarah Hawthorne—at Hawthorne Hill. Everyone knows it. It's the biggest cotton plantation in Virginia." She paused, and a faint pink crept up to her cheeks. "Well, perhaps you should direct your letter to my mama. I am not accustomed to getting letters, you see."

"Of course." She looked very young, hardly sixteen.

"And perhaps you should not mention Willie by name," she went on, "especially if you take him north." Her gaze scoured his face. "You do come from the North, don't you?"

"Yes, I do."

"And you know that in some Northern states slavery is illegal?"

"I know," he said. "But this boy is too young to be on his own. I'll keep him with me 'til he gets older."

What on earth was he doing, digging himself in deeper and deeper? He could have asked the chief where to send the boy, to people who'd care for him. Now he'd committed himself to taking care of him. And there would be no weaseling out of it either. When Calvin Sharp made a promise, he kept it. So, it looked as if he was in for the long haul.

But when he looked into the misty violet eyes of Sarah Hawthorne, he couldn't even feel regret at his actions. Meeting her made up for everything. How had such a beautiful, compassionate creature grown up in this part of the country?

"I must go," she said, casting an anxious glance in the direction of the overseer. "Mama will want to know what happened. She's waiting at the Exchange Hotel. She was feeling poorly today and so didn't come along. Thank you again, Mr. Sharp."

He resisted the impulse to reach out and take her little hand in his, instead contenting himself with saying, "Miss Hawthorne?"

"Yes?"

"If I were to come by the plantation, to—ah—discuss matters of business, would your father take my arrival amiss?"

She sighed. "Not as long as you're a firm supporter of slavery." Her eyes said more than the words. "Papa doesn't care for anyone trifling with our way of life. He fully supports the Fugitive Slave Law."

"I understand," he said.

She peered at him. "Tell me, Mr. Sharp, do you ever travel on the good ship *Zion?*"

Ship? Odd question. What had ships to do with this? He shrugged. "A ship called *Zion?* No, afraid not. Never heard of it. Why do you ask?"

A sigh escaped the slave girl, but she remained otherwise silent.

"Nothing," Miss Hawthorne muttered, turning away.

A few paces away she paused and smiled back at the boy. "You'll be a good boy for Mr. Sharp, Willie. I know it."

"Yes'um, Miss Sarah. I do my bestest."

Then she was gone. And Calvin grew aware of a faint scent of gardenia that hung in the stale air. But almost as soon as he recognized it, it was gone. And all he could smell was the stench of unwashed bodies mingled with the odor of fear.

He heard a little sigh from beside him and looked down,

just in time to see the boy keel over. Muttering under his breath, Calvin picked up his slave and made his way out of the auction rooms. *A barbarous ungodly place, the South.* The sooner he was out of it, the better.

two

Back at the Exchange Hotel, Sarah slipped out of her bonnet and shawl and hurried to where Mama rested on the chaise. "It's all right," Sarah told her. "A Northerner bought him. Willie's safe."

Mama sighed in relief, the lines in her tired face smoothing out a little. "Thank the good Lord! Oh, how I've prayed."

"I been praying, too," Minta said. "Prayers don't always help. But this time they did! Praise the Lord Jesus. Willie's gonna be all right. I feel it in my bones."

"The man," Mama said anxiously, "the man who bought Willie. Did anyone know his name?"

Sarah hesitated. What she'd done seemed very unladylike now, though at the time it had seemed quite natural. "I spoke to him, Mama. He was a stranger." She pitched her voice lower. "A Northerner. I–I thanked him."

Mama frowned. "A stranger. You shouldn't—"

"We were so afraid, Minta and I. Beau's papa was bidding on Willie. And you know how *he* is."

Mama sighed again. Everyone knew how hard Reginald Gordon was on his slaves.

"The man who bought Willie is named Calvin," Sarah went on. "Calvin Sharp. H–he offered to write to you, to tell us how Willie was faring." She reached out to touch Minta's arm. Poor Minta had been so worried. And so had she. It was awful not being able to help someone you loved.

Mama glanced around the comfortable hotel sitting room,

13

looking at the door as though someone could be hiding on the other side, listening to them. Sarah nodded to Minta, and she padded across the room and quietly opened the door to the hall. There was no one there. She stepped out and looked both ways. Then she came back in, nodded, and shut the door. Perhaps it was silly to take such precautions, but they had to be careful. Many lives depended on them.

Still, though the hall had been empty, Mama's whisper could barely be heard. "Is he—? Did you ask—?"

Sarah shook her head. "I don't think he's knows much about the Underground, Mama. He didn't seem to know the code about the good ship *Zion*."

Mama sighed again.

"But he's a good man," Sarah went on. "He said, he asked, if he could stop by to visit. If Papa would mind."

Mama's eyes opened wide in alarm. "He mustn't—"

"I warned him, Mama. I told him Papa is a big slavery man."

Mama struggled upright. "If your father ever finds out, if he ever discovers that we've been helping runaways all these years, he'll—" She fell back, unable to go on, her face even paler than usual.

"Don't you worry none, Missus," Minta said, her dark eyes full of compassion. "If Massa finds out what we done, Minta take the blame. Minta take it all."

"But, Minta—" Sarah began.

Minta shrugged. "If he ever find out we helping runaways, he *know* I be in on it. He sell me South anyway. If he don't kill me." She shrugged. "No matter. Willie safe now." She sighed. "If only I could get Hiram to follow the North Star to freedom. I worry so 'bout that man."

"Hiram will be careful," Sarah said, though she worried

about him too. "He loves you. And you know he won't leave you."

That made Minta smile. "He don't love me no more than I love him." She turned to Mama. "I go get you your afternoon tea, Missus." And she went down to the hotel kitchen.

"I'm going to rest 'til Minta gets back," Mama said with a little smile, and closed her eyes.

"Good." Sarah put a kiss on her cheek. "I'll be in the bedroom. Maybe I'll lie on the bed for a while."

In the bedroom, she dropped her bonnet and shawl on the chair. Strange how she could remember Mr. Sharp so plainly. Calvin Sharp. She repeated his name softly to herself.

Mrs. Calvin Sharp. Goodness! Now she was being plain silly. Mr. Sharp probably had a wife. And even if he didn't, *she* was promised to Beau, had been ever since they were babies. If only Beau's father weren't so hard on his slaves, harder even than Papa. And Beau was just as bad as his father. She'd heard him boast about having slaves beaten for the littlest infraction of the rules. Or sending them off to the slave breaker just because they didn't obey fast enough.

She sighed. How could she stand before God and vow to love and honor a man like that? She could never promise to obey him. She had promised to obey God—God who loved Minta and Willie and Hiram as much as He loved Beau and Mr. Gordon. Though why God should love such cruel people as them was hard to understand. But the Bible said it was so.

God didn't care about the color of a person's skin or the evil a person had done but had sent His Son to save them all. "Neither bond nor free," the Bible said. God made no distinctions about people.

Did Calvin Sharp believe that? He had seemed like a good man, a kind man. A man needn't believe in God to find slavery disgraceful, though that was more often the case. She hoped Calvin Sharp believed. She hoped he knew the comfort of a heavenly Father.

She slid her slippers off and lay back on the bed, closing her eyes against the sunlight filtering in through the lacy curtains. She'd known even before he spoke that Mr. Sharp wasn't a Southerner. Something about the way he stood there, an intensity to his movements, made him different from the men she knew. She could still see his face. The hardness to the jut of his jaw, the angular look to the planes of his handsome face. Well, not exactly handsome, but attractive anyway. Very attractive.

And when she'd peered up into his dark eyes—everything about him was dark in a way, his eyes, his hair, even his skin—she could see pain there. He had endured some terrible hardship, some hardship that had molded him into the formidable man he was. And yet he wasn't all granite. He'd bought Willie, been kind to the child. Somehow he had come to understand that the evil of slavery must be battled.

"Dear Lord," she prayed. "Please keep Mr. Sharp and Willie safe." She took a deep breath. "And if it be Your will, let me see them both again."

three

Hawthorne Hill—December 1859

That cold afternoon the road north from Richmond was empty except for a single horseman bundled against the chill wind, a small black boy riding pillion behind him, and the packhorse that trailed them.

"Warm enough?" Calvin asked, glancing over his shoulder.

"Yes, Massa. Nice 'n' warm. But I kin walk. I strong now."

Calvin smiled. Two months had made some changes in the boy. Besides being cleaner, he was heavier. He hardly looked like the scrawny child Calvin had plucked off the auction block. But there was no point in the boy walking when Runner could easily carry double.

They rode in silence for some minutes more.

"Massa?"

"Yes, Willie?"

"We really going to Hawthorne Hill?"

"Yes."

Willie was silent, but the clasp of his arms tightened around Calvin's waist.

"Why do you ask?"

"Well, I wants to see Minta. And Miss Sarah. And Missus. But—"

"Whoa, Runner." He reined up and half turned so he

17

could see the boy's face. There was fear in Willie's eyes, something he hadn't seen there for weeks now.

"Remember what I told you, Willie, when we went after Josiah Cooper?"

Willie nodded, his face somber. "Yes, Massa. I 'member. Pinkerton men gets scared just like everybody else. But they does their jobs anyway."

"Right. Now, no one is going to hurt you at Hawthorne Hill. No one. I'll see to that. You're my partner, and partners always look out for each other."

"Right," Willie said, his grin reappearing. "I'll 'member that."

"Good."

Calvin set Runner to walking again. Would Miss Hawthorne be as beautiful as he remembered her? Had she included him in her prayers as he'd included her in his? Had she dreamed dreams like his?

Of course not. His dreams were foolish. A man who'd come up from Chicago's slums, even if he was now a respected Pinkerton operative, had no business dreaming about marriage to a Southern belle. But he was going to see her at least. His heart beat faster in anticipation.

With Josiah Cooper and his gang jailed and their counterfeiting days over, it was time to head north again. But not before he looked once more into Sarah Hawthorne's beautiful face. The chief had telegraphed that he didn't have to start back until after Christmas. That gave him a few days to get to know—

"Massa. Up there. That the way to Hawthorne Hill."

Calvin turned Runner into the avenue of oaks. Tall and stately, they towered over the road that led up the slight hill to the gleaming white plantation house. Calvin sucked in a breath. He'd seen many plantation houses in the last months, but none finer or more magnificent. This place could have housed the inhabitants of several blocks of Chicago tenements.

Runner reached the steps to the huge front veranda. A slave boy came running up to attend to the horses. He stood there, his eyes growing bigger. "Willie?" he squeaked. "Willie, that you?"

Willie dropped lightly to the ground. His chest puffed out. "Yeah, Joe. It's me. We come to visit."

Calvin smiled to himself. Joe looked properly impressed by Willie's finery.

Calvin swung down and turned to the now waiting butler. "I am Calvin Sharp," he said. "I've come to discuss business with the colonel."

"Yes, sir," the black butler said. "Right this way, please. The colonel is away just now, but the Missus will want to see you."

Calvin looked at Willie. "You can go with Joe if you want. Or you can go look for your sister."

The butler's mask of dignity slipped a little, and a twinkle appeared in his eyes. "Minta is with Miss Sarah, sir, in the east parlor. I'll tell Miss Sarah you're here."

"Thank you," Calvin said.

Willie turned to Joe. "After I sees Minta, I come down to the stable and see you."

Joe nodded. "Why you wearing boots?" he asked, his glance going to Willie's feet.

"We going north," Willie said. "Massa say it gets real cold up there. I gonna need 'em."

"North?" Joe whispered, rolling his eyes from side to side. "You going north?"

"Yes," Willie said. "Massa work for the Pinkerton Detective Agency. In Chicago it is."

"Joe," the butler interrupted. "You quit that talking and get the gentleman's horses taken care of."

"I going," Joe said.

"This way, sir," the butler said. "You can wait in the west parlor."

In the east parlor, Sarah set another stitch in her needlepoint and shifted in her chair. At least Mama looked better today, not quite so pale. Beside her, Minta sat on a low stool, sorting the colors of wool.

Sarah sighed and stopped stitching for a moment. She'd been so restless lately, ever since that last trip to Richmond. Papa had been pressing her, too, about marrying Beau, saying it was time she gave him the grandson he wanted, the future master of Hawthorne Hill.

The thought made cold shivers creep up her spine. She didn't want to give Papa any babies to raise up to be slave owners. And besides, if she left Hawthorne Hill, Papa would send Minta with her. That would take Minta away from her Hiram.

And what about Mama? Her health had been failing. Today she looked pretty good, but she'd been having more and more bad days, days when she could barely get dressed and move about. Still, as long as she could walk, Mama would not give up helping runaways.

No, Sarah thought, *I have to stay at Hawthorne Hill as long as possible. Mama needs me.* So far Papa had given in to her because in his own way, he did love Mama, and he could see she wasn't well. And, of course, he knew nothing about their helping anyone.

But it was hard to tell how long Beau could be held off.

He'd been getting more and more bossy, ordering her about as if she were some slave, or already his wife. Another shiver traveled down her spine. She had no desire to be anyone's wife, least of all Beau's. Marriage had been instituted by God. And it was not meant to be entered into lightly.

Albert appeared in the doorway. "A visitor, Missus. A Mr. Sharp to see the colonel. He's waiting in the west parlor."

In surprise Sarah looked down at the drop of blood rising where she'd just stuck her finger with the needle. Mr. Sharp! Here! Her prayers had been answered.

Mama nodded. "Show him in here," she said.

Sarah swallowed hard, trying to slow the pounding of her heart. She'd been so silly, indulging in those schoolgirl's daydreams about Mr. Sharp. Probably he wasn't at all as she remembered him.

Minta leaned over from her stool to press a scrap of cloth over the punctured finger. "Thank you," Sarah said, but her eyes were on the door.

Had Mr. Sharp brought Willie? Surely he wouldn't have come here without him, not after he'd promised.

And then Mr. Sharp was there, standing in the doorway, looking even better than she remembered. And his dark eyes shone with an emotion that looked almost like joy.

"Mr. Sharp," she said, remembering her manners. "How good to see you again."

He crossed the room and bent to take her hand. "The pleasure is mine, Miss Hawthorne." He gazed into her eyes until she thought she must be blushing.

"Minta! Miss Sarah! Look a' me!"

And there was Willie, a clean, smiling Willie who looked as if he'd grown a few inches and added on more than a few pounds since she saw him last, and wearing new pants and boots.

"Willie!" Minta swiped at her eyes with the back of her hand.

"Don't cry, Minta," Willie said. "Massa take good care of me. Look." And he paraded his finery for them before Minta led him off to a corner to talk.

"Sit down, Mr. Sharp," Mama said.

"Thank you."

Mr. Sharp settled in the chair next to Sarah's. His nearness made her feel giddy, as if he'd been smelling too many magnolias in full bloom.

"I understand you have business with the colonel," Mama said.

Mr. Sharp nodded. "I am an operative with the Pinkerton Detective Agency," he said. "I have been trailing some counterfeiters."

Mama paled slightly. "Aren't such men dangerous?"

Mr. Sharp shrugged. "Perhaps. At times. But these men have been put away. They won't be able to hurt anyone for some time."

Mama looked relieved. "That's good."

"What did they counterfeit?" Sarah asked.

"Banknotes on one of Chicago's banks. We were hired to stop them. And we did."

Mama nodded as though she heard of such things every day. "Then what is your business with my husband?"

Sarah glanced at her in surprise. It wasn't like Mama to be so forward with a stranger.

"Nothing vital," Mr. Sharp said evenly. "I just wanted to inquire if the colonel had run across any false banknotes or heard of anyone who had." He nodded toward the corner where Minta and Willie were talking. "I thought the boy might like to see his sister again."

His gaze sought Sarah's. "I also thought you'd want to know how he was faring."

"I did," she said, wondering why his smile should be so much nicer than Beau's. Why did she feel so comfortable with Mr. Sharp, a man she hardly knew, and so uncomfortable with Beau, the man she was supposed to spend the rest of her life with?

Mr. Sharp nodded. "It's my—"

"Mr. Sharp. How do you do?" Papa stood in the doorway. Mama shrank back into herself as she usually did when he was near, and in the corner Minta and Willie grew silent, but Mr. Sharp wasn't intimidated. He got to his feet and crossed the room to where Papa stood.

"Hello, Colonel," he said, extending his hand. "I'm pleased to meet you. I've heard many good things about Hawthorne Hill."

"Indeed," Papa said. "Come along to my office and tell me what you've heard."

As Papa led Mr. Sharp out and down the hall, Sarah prayed, *Please, God, don't let Mr. Sharp say anything that will make Papa suspicious.*

four

The well-furnished room the colonel led Calvin into was obviously a business office. In addition to the door they'd come through, it had another door to the outside, now closed to the wind. Ledgers sat in orderly rows on shelves along one wall. Calvin thought of Willie and the thousands like him whose life and death meant nothing but figures in those ledgers to men like the colonel. How could a man who called himself Christian enslave others?

Calvin sighed. Somehow he'd figured that a man who could so callously dispose of a child like Willie would look like the monster he was. But the colonel looked like the retired military man he claimed to be—tall and lean, with only a slight sprinkle of gray to his temples, and a preciseness of movement that belied the slow drawl of his speech.

"Sit down, sit down," the colonel said jovially, settling himself behind a huge burnished desk. "You come from up North, I hear."

Calvin nodded, easing himself into a chair. This was the tricky part—to tell the truth but not all of it. He was a God-fearing man, and he didn't like deceiving people. But surely God would forgive him for trying to protect the innocent.

"So," the colonel said, leaning back in his chair. "Tell me what business brings you here."

And Calvin launched into his prepared story about Josiah Cooper and the counterfeit banknotes, about tracing the man and his gang to the auction rooms and deciding to buy

Willie. It was all true. And thank the good Lord a man wasn't constrained to reveal the motives for his actions.

"I finally caught up with Cooper," he concluded. "And he and his helpers have been sent to prison for a good long time. Now I'm calling on planters hereabouts to see if anyone's noticed any other banknote irregularities. Or knows anyone who has."

It was all true, even to the calling on other planters. He'd stopped at other places on the way here, and he'd asked his questions.

"I see," the colonel said. "Well now, let me think on it for a bit." He opened an inlaid box on the desk. "Care for a cheroot?"

"No, thank you," Calvin said. "I find it better for my profession to abstain. And Mr. Pinkerton agrees. The need for a smoke can give a man away."

"Sound reasoning." The colonel gazed at him from eyes as dark as Sarah's, but without their compassion. He selected a cheroot and lit it, leaned back and propped his dusty boots on the desk.

Footsteps echoed on the veranda and a sharp rap sounded on the outside door.

The colonel looked over. "Come in."

The door opened to reveal the overseer. He was minus the vermilion waistcoat, but otherwise looked much the same. Disreputable and dirty. "Colonel?" he whined.

"Yes, Vickers." The colonel waved a hand. "What is it?"

Vickers stepped in and closed the door. "It's Brutus, Colonel. He's been shirking again. Hasn't done his work right fer a couple days."

The colonel raised an eyebrow. "I thought you had him beaten last week."

"I did indeed," Vickers said. "Had Hiram give him the lash. Didn't do him no good, though. That Brutus just plain lazy."

The colonel shrugged. "Then send him to Jenkins the slave breaker for a few weeks. He'll work after that."

Vickers grinned evilly. "Right, Colonel. That he will. I'll send him off today."

Calvin looked down—his hands were curving into fists. He shoved them into his pockets. He couldn't hit the overseer, much as he might want to. There was nothing he could do to help this particular slave. But when he got back North, he was going to do a lot more to get rid of the despicable institution of slavery.

Vickers backed out and closed the door, and Calvin swallowed his rage. Slavery would not survive. Sooner or later, such a terrible thing had to fail.

The colonel puffed on his cheroot and said, "Vickers drinks too much, but he makes the slaves produce. This is a business, after all. And production is what makes it worthwhile."

"I suppose so," Calvin managed to say.

"Looking for counterfeit banknotes, eh?" the colonel said, as though Vickers had never stood there, as though no slave had ever been beaten.

Calvin swallowed hard. He had to get along with the colonel. He was a guest in the man's house. And, besides, a Pinkerton man knew when to hold his peace. "Yes, sir. We think we've found most of them. But there are always counterfeiters around, looking for an easy way to get money."

The colonel shook his head. "The criminal things men will do."

"Yes, sir," Calvin managed to mutter.

The colonel took another puff. "Can't say as I've heard of any problems with banknotes around here. Probably would have if there'd been any."

"I'm glad to hear you've had no problems," Calvin said, though he'd been hoping for an excuse—any excuse—to stay at Hawthorne Hill, to stay near Sarah. He wasn't sure when he'd started thinking of her as "Sarah" instead of "Miss Hawthorne," but he had, and he'd better be careful. The colonel might offer a Pinkerton man the famed Southern hospitality, but he would never regard such a man as a suitable son-in-law. He wouldn't stand for a Northern upstart romancing his only daughter.

Puffing on his cheroot, the colonel stared thoughtfully into the distance. "Still, though I haven't heard anything, maybe you should spend the holidays with us while I ask around." He shifted his gaze to Calvin. "Unless you have to go right off on another assignment."

Calvin gulped. How had this happened? Did he dare to think that God was working for him? That his buying Willie had had another purpose besides rescuing the child? "I don't have to start back 'til after Christmas, sir."

"Good. Then you can relax and enjoy yourself. We'll be going to church tomorrow. I'll introduce you to folks. Then the Gordons will be coming for dinner. Reginald Gordon and his son Beau. Beau is promised to my daughter. They'll be spending the holidays with us here at Hawthorne Hill."

And you're giving me warning, Calvin thought, keeping his face calm. *Warning me that she's out of bounds.* "It's very kind of you to invite me," he said. "I would enjoy the rest."

The colonel's boots hit the floor. He ground out his cheroot beneath a boot heel and left it there on the polished wood floor. For a slave to clean up, no doubt. "I'll see you at dinner then."

Calvin got to his feet, too. He had definitely been dismissed. "Thank you, sir."

The colonel shrugged. "I'm sure the ladies will enjoy your company."

Calvin barely kept his features from revealing his surprise. Could the man suspect something? "The ladies, sir?"

The colonel smiled, the indulgent smile of a doting father. "Yes, my wife and daughter appreciated your purchasing Willie." His voice was cordial, but his eyes skewered Calvin. "You know how ladies are. They have soft hearts, no head for business." He laughed, but Calvin heard no humor in the sound. "Give the ladies a free hand and we'd end up in the poorhouse."

Calvin nodded. It was the most he could do given the anger storming through him. This man really believed himself to be a caring human being. He really believed that his wife and daughter were misguided because they thought of slaves as human beings with feelings.

Calvin turned to the inner door. "I've been a long time on the road, sir." If he didn't get out of here, away from this hypocrite, he was going to explode. "Perhaps I'll rest for a while."

five

The next morning when Calvin joined the colonel and his family for church services, Willie stood in the back with Minta and the other slaves.

Calvin sat in the pew beside the colonel, not beside Sarah where he wanted to be. The colonel and his wife were both between them, as was only right and proper, Calvin knew. But that didn't stop him from wanting, from wishing that he had the right to sit beside Sarah, for all the world to see. Sitting across the table from her at dinner last night had only made him admire her beauty more, wish more for the chance to get to know her. But it didn't seem likely.

Sorry, Lord. I know I should be listening to the sermon, not thinking about Sarah, even though my thoughts of her are most respectable.

Calvin looked to the pulpit. The clergyman was a short man, almost as round as he was tall. *But a man's looks,* Calvin reminded himself, *have little to do with his standing in the eyes of the Lord.*

"Brothers and sisters," the preacher was saying, "I ask you, didn't the Lord tell us to be good servants?" In front of Calvin, heads nodded in agreement. "Oh, yes, He did," the preacher went on. "And when you neglect your duties, when you're impudent and saucy—what does this mean?"

Impudent? Saucy? To God? Calvin couldn't imagine being either to the God his mother had raised him to believe

29

in. A man did his duty, however irksome it might be, because the Lord had laid it on him. Just as Mother had done her duty, raising the family after his drunken father had been killed.

"When you do wrong toward master and mistress, why—" the preacher went on, "why, that's sin. The worst sin of all."

Calvin swallowed, hard. This sermon wasn't even addressed to the planters. It was meant for slaves! To think that a man of God—or at least a man who claimed to be a man of God—could preach such infamy.

But the preacher went on. "When you do wrong to the master or mistress, you're doing wrong against God Himself." He glared at the slaves clustered along the back wall. "Yes, sir. Against God Himself. Master and mistress were put over you by God. A divine institution. He 'spects you to do your duty by them. To obey them. And if you don't, God'll punish you. He'll punish you for your sins." He brought a fist down on the pulpit. "That He will. And it'll be bad, worse than anything you can imagine. Fire and brimstone, that's what it'll be! Burning forever—in fire and brimstone!"

A murmur went through the gathered slaves. Calvin dug his nails into his palms. How cruel. To enslave people and then use fear of the Almighty to keep them in line. That the God who had sent His only Son to free men from sin should be used in such a perverted way made Calvin's bile rise. Christ had been outraged at the buying and selling in the temple courts. And that had been only animals. How much more would this have angered Him!

But Calvin sat on, schooling himself to silence. There was nothing he could do here, but once he got North he was going to become an active member of the Anti-Slavery League. He was going to fight this evil until it was completely eradicated. *I promise, Lord. And I'll leave manumission papers for Willie, too. In case something happens to me. He's never going to be a slave. Never.*

The rest of the service passed slowly, but finally it was over and they filed out. Calvin made himself shake the hand of the fat little minister, who was perspiring profusely, and even managed to mumble something about an interesting sermon. A good thing Pinkerton trained his operatives to keep their true feelings hidden.

Then the colonel began introductions. Calvin couldn't begin to remember all the names and faces. But he recognized one face, one he'd never forget. The fat, slovenly planter who'd bid on Willie was Reginald Gordon. Calvin wasn't likely to forget the man or the menace in his eyes. Gordon's wife, a slight woman dressed entirely in a pale gray almost the color of her skin, was practically invisible. Their son, the Beau who would someday, God forbid, be Sarah's husband, was tall and well dressed, with broad shoulders and curly blond hair. His only resemblance to his father was in the eyes—they exuded the same steely menace. Beauregard Gordon was not a man to thwart—those eyes said so plainly.

Watching him take Sarah's hand, Calvin discovered in his heart an unchristian urge to do the man physical damage. *Forgive me, Lord,* he prayed. But the urge was still there.

Sarah smiled at Beau and withdrew her fingers from his. Was it just wishful thinking on his part, Calvin asked himself, or did she really edge a little away from her intended? But why should she? The man was personable enough. He could take good care of her. And she *was* Southern raised.

True, she cared about Willie and his sister. But she was the colonel's daughter. So she probably held for slavery, too. Calvin sighed. It was time for him to face reality. All the hard work in the world couldn't bring him an inch closer to making Sarah Hawthorne love him. Or keep him from loving her.

Later that day, Calvin looked around the colonel's dining room table. Besides the Gordons and the fat little minister, there were some others whose names he couldn't remember.

"That's stupid," Beau's father said, wiping gravy from his chin. "Nigras don't need to read. Just makes 'em uppity. Gives 'em ideas they don't need. You take what happened at Harper's Ferry this October last."

Mrs. Gordon shivered and grew even paler. "Mr. Gordon," Mrs. Hawthorne said, glancing her way and back to Beau's father. "Perhaps we should talk about something else. Your wife—"

"My wife knows her place," Mr. Gordon said. "She'll keep to it."

Mrs. Hawthorne opened her mouth and closed it again without speaking. Calvin wondered how she had survived this long in such a climate.

"They hanged John Brown," the colonel said. "And rightly so. Though hanging was too good a fate for a man who instigated a slave rebellion."

"I've heard that he was insane," the preacher said. And heads nodded in agreement.

Calvin nodded, too. For once he was in agreement with these people. Brown must have been crazy to believe that a slave rebellion would lead to the end of slavery. Instead it had led to harder and more repressive measures.

He cast a quick glance in Sarah's direction. She was across the table and down from him, Beau at her side, of course. What was she thinking? How could she have grown up with any compassion at all, raised with sentiments like these?

"Maybe Dr. Cartwright's theories are correct," Beau said, looking at Calvin.

Calvin took the bait. "I'm afraid I'm not familiar with Dr. Cartwright's theories."

Beau smiled and Calvin's hackles rose. Beau already had Sarah; the man needn't look at him with such obvious condescension. "Let me see if I can summarize it for you. And the ladies." He patted Sarah's hand. "Dr. Cartwright says the nigras run away because they suffer from a mental illness. Drapetomania, he calls it. He says the illness is common to nigras and cats. In our cold climate, the nigra brain tends to freeze, inducing insanity."

Again heads nodded in agreement.

"I see," Calvin said. And indeed he did. He saw that these people would grasp at anything, even the most ridiculous claptrap, to justify the enslavement of those on whose labor their life of luxury was based.

The colonel's gaze was on him, his eyes steely. "Ever own a slave before, Mr. Sharp?"

"No, sir," Calvin replied. "In my business they aren't real useful." Another lie. But no one at this table would believe that Willie—Willie who couldn't read or write and was only seven years old—had been instrumental in helping him catch Cooper and his cronies. But it was true.

Sarah looked at him, her dark eyes pleading. He wanted to reassure her that he wouldn't divulge her secret, but he couldn't, so he went on, telling the truth—just not all of it.

"It's nice to have a boy, though. To do for me."

The colonel smiled. "Long as you don't let him learn to read."

"I hadn't thought about it," Calvin said truthfully. But he was thinking about it now. Oh, yes, the minute he got the boy away from here, Willie was going to learn to read! *I promise it, God.*

six

Late that evening Calvin reached his room. The strain of pretending to agree with these people combined with that of hiding his feelings for Sarah had left him drained. With relief he saw that Willie had laid out his night things. Generally, he traveled light while on assignment, but a trip of this duration required some luggage. A Pinkerton operative was always neat and clean, unless his assignment demanded otherwise.

As usual, Willie had put out the worn Bible, the one physical possession Mother had left him when she passed on to her heavenly reward. After Calvin was ready for bed, Willie stripped off his own clothes and laid them carefully to one side, his boots precisely aligned. The boy did love those boots. Then he wriggled into his old homespun shirt, now clean and serving as a nightshirt, and sat cross-legged on the quilts that made up his bed. "What story you reading me from the Good Book tonight, Massa?" he asked, his face eager.

Calvin smiled, the first genuine smile of this difficult day. He picked up the Bible and settled into the room's comfortable chair. "Tonight's story is about a king."

"Ain't no kings here," Willie said.

"Right," Calvin agreed. "This king lived a long time ago. Far away. In a place called Egypt. He was called the pharaoh."

"Massa! Minta taught it me."

Calvin nodded. "Then why don't you tell it?"

Willie straightened his nightshirt and sang softly.

> "When Israel was in Egypt's land,
>   Let my people go.
> Oppressed so hard they could not stand,
>   Let my people go.
> Go down, Moses,
>   'Way down in Egypt's land.
> Tell ole Pharaoh,
>   To let my people go."

When the boy finished, Calvin said, "That's very good, Willie."

Willie crossed the room to peer into the Bible. "Where the story in there?"

Calvin pointed. "It starts here."

Willie heaved a sigh. "Wisht I could read."

Calvin opened his arms. "Climb up here on my knee and I'll show you the letters."

"Can't, Massa." Willie's eyes widened. "Slaves ain't 'llowed to read." He glanced at the door as if he expected it to burst open and reveal the colonel, ready to drag him away. "And they puts you in jail."

Calvin shrugged. "Will *you* tell them?"

Willie made a face. "Oh no, Massa. Willie don't tell."

"Then come on."

Willie climbed into his lap. "Now, Willie," Calvin said, looking into the dark eyes so near his own. "First, remember we're partners."

Willie nodded. "Partners. I 'members."

"Now, supposing we're on a job, like when we were

after that counterfeiter, Cooper. And supposing I need to send you a message—a secret important message. How could I do it?"

Willie shook his head. "Don't know, Massa. How?"

"Well, if you could read, it would be easy."

Willie considered this, his dark face thoughtful. "I got to learn to read," he said finally, nodding. "But I won't tell no one. Never. Not even Minta."

"Good," Calvin said. "Then that's settled. We'll start by learning the letters. Now, this is an *A*."

"A," Willie repeated, staring at it. "And there's one, too." He pointed with his finger. "And there's 'nother."

"Right. You watch for the *As*," Calvin said, "and I'll read the story." And he began reading Exodus 5:1-2, " 'And afterward Moses and Aaron went in, and told Pharaoh, "Thus saith the LORD God of Israel, 'Let my people go, that they may hold a feast unto me in the wilderness.' " And Pharaoh said, "Who is the LORD, that I should obey his voice to let Israel go? I know not the LORD, neither will I let Israel go." ' "

&

On the other side of the great house, Sarah sat in front of her dressing table while Minta brushed her hair the required one hundred strokes. The nightly ritual was a comforting one for Sarah, a time for her and Minta to talk.

"Willie looking real good," Minta said, her words timed to her strokes. "Mr. Sharp, he a good man. I pray for him, Miss Sarah. I pray for him and Willie both. Every night."

Sarah smoothed her nightgown over her knees. "Me too, Minta. I have ever since that day at the auction house."

Minta's gaze met hers in the mirror. "Mr. Sharp, he a nice-looking man. Got a good heart, too. Too bad you promised to Mr. Beau."

Sarah felt the heat creep up to redden her cheeks. "Why, Minta. Whatever makes you say a thing like that?"

Minta laughed the deep, throaty laugh that was hers alone. "I seen how Mr. Sharp, he look at you. I seen."

What if Papa had seen? Sarah's skin went cold. She thought her heart might pound its way right out of her chest. "Oh, Minta! Do you think Papa saw? Do you think Papa knows?"

Minta's dark hands came to rest on Sarah's shoulders, holding her on the stool, calming her. "Now, Miss Sarah, don't you go worrying yourself none. The colonel, he ain't gonna pay no mind to a Yankee man. He know you a good girl. You ain't marrying no Yankee. He can rest easy 'bout that."

As always, Minta's soothing made Sarah feel better. "Thank you, Minta. I know you're right. Papa won't even think of Mr. Sharp as a prospective husband. I wish it wasn't so, but it is." She knew she was blushing again. "I *do* like Mr. Sharp. I like him very much." She turned toward Minta, watching her face. "Do you really think he likes me—like that?"

"I knows it," Minta said firmly. "He got that same look when he look at you that my Hiram got when he look at me. That loving look." She laughed again. "Mr. Sharp, he taken with you, all right. Question is—what you gonna do 'bout it?"

"Do?" Sarah whispered, her heart pounding. "What can I do? I'm promised to Beau. Ever since we were babies, we've been promised."

"I knows that." Minta raised an eyebrow. "You loving Mr. Beau?"

Sarah shook her head. "Of course I don't love him. How could I? You've heard the stories—how cruel he is to his slaves." She shuddered. "And look at the way his father treats his mother. It's just awful."

Minta nodded solemnly. "I knows."

Sarah shivered. "I don't want to marry Beau. I never have. But, Minta, what can I do?"

Minta looked thoughtful. "If I was you, Miss Sarah," she said. "I'd pray hard. Real hard."

Later, after Minta had gone back to Slave Row for the night, Sarah read her Bible. Then she knelt beside the bed and bowed her head. "Dear Father in heaven," she prayed, "I know the Bible tells us to honor our parents. But I don't want to marry Beau. He's cruel. He frightens me so. I know Papa wants me to marry Beau, *expects* me to marry Beau. But Mama doesn't want me to marry him. She knows how I feel about him. She's afraid of him, too. I'm sorry to be disobeying Papa, but I have to help the run-aways. I know that's what You want me to do."

She shivered there on her knees and pulled her shawl tighter around her shoulders. "I think very highly of Mr. Sharp, God. He's a good Christian man. But You know that. You know how I feel about everything. I think I would like to be Mr. Sharp's wife. But if that isn't possible, God, at least don't let me belong to Beau." Her whole body went cold. "I know it's a terrible sin to say so, but I would rather die, God, than be Beau's wife. I really would. When he touches me, I feel sick inside. So sick."

She swallowed hard. "And please bless Mama and Papa, and Minta and her Hiram, and Mr. Sharp and Willie. And whatever happens, Your will be done."

Climbing into bed, Sarah snuggled down under the

covers. God hadn't appeared to her in a burning bush or a pillar of fire, but still she felt He had heard her prayers. Mama was praying, too, she knew, that the marriage to Beau would never take place. And back in the slave cabins, Minta was doing the same. Surely their prayers would be answered. Surely God would help her escape marriage to Beau. And if He didn't—well, there would be time to think about that later.

She wanted to think about other things now. There were still a couple days 'til Christmas, a couple days before Mr. Sharp had to start north again. A couple days more of his smile, of his pleasant conversation, of— She would think of *that*, not of how she would miss him when he was gone.

Christmas was going to be a busy time. Beside all the usual festivities, the baking and the decorating, the kissing ball and wreaths, the swags and the hanging of the greens, the songs and the guests and the gifts, there would be Minta's wedding to Hiram. Of course, it wouldn't be a real wedding with a minister. Papa thought that was unnecessary for slaves. But Minta had said, "It all right, Miss Sarah. Lord Jesus know our hearts. He know we be truly married."

There might not be a minister, but there would be a feast, the best feast Sarah and Mama could arrange. All the slaves on the plantation would be there, eating and dancing and laughing. And Minta and Hiram would be together at last.

Sarah sighed. Together. That was what married meant— being together. She'd never wanted to be married before. How could she when she saw how Mama was afraid of Papa? When she saw how Beau's mother was afraid of Mr. Gordon? When *she* herself was afraid of Beau?

But it was different now. She could see that being married might be good. She smiled there in the darkened room. She wasn't afraid of Mr. Sharp. He would never hurt her. She didn't know how she knew that, but she knew it. She was as sure of him as she was of Mama—or Minta. And knowing that, she asked the Lord once more to keep him safe, and drifted off to sleep.

seven

The days before Christmas passed quickly, far too quickly, Calvin thought. But there was nothing he could do to slow them down. So he did the best he could and left the rest in God's hands.

He certainly had no desire to observe the inner workings of plantation life. But the colonel and Beau, who would presumably one day be the master of Hawthorne Hill's slaves as well as his own, seemed to glory in showing off every revolting detail of how they achieved their ill-gotten gains.

They rode out to see the cotton fields; they toured the various outbuildings; they walked down Slave Row, inspecting cabins; they paused to watch a slave being disciplined, a scene that had Calvin gritting his teeth and shoving his hands deep in his pockets. But just as bad as having to nod and pretend that he admired the running of the plantation was the fact that he was not able to spend these precious hours with Sarah. He wanted to get to know her better, to discover what was important to her. But they had little time to talk—and they were never alone.

With the other guests, he helped put up the Christmas decorations—the swags and wreaths, the garlands and ribbons, and the tree decorated with strung popcorn and paper ornaments, the many trappings of wealth and comfort that had never graced his childhood home.

And the kissing ball. They put up a kissing ball of twined

mistletoe. Of course, Beau had made use of it as soon as possible, catching Sarah under it almost at once and giving her a kiss that made Calvin want to tear the man limb from limb. He didn't, of course. A Pinkerton agent knew how to control his anger, as well as his other emotions. And of course, such sentiments were unchristian.

But he was glad to see that from that moment on Sarah avoided going near the kissing ball. It meant, of course, that he couldn't avail himself of the liberty it offered, but it also meant that Beau didn't get any more chances. He was sorry to think so—it was unchristian, too—but a more obnoxious human being had never entered Calvin's life. Still, Beau and his family were invited guests, just as he was, so Calvin swallowed his disgust and did his best to tolerate their company.

He did manage a few minutes with Sarah when the colonel lit the Yule log. As a collected ahhhh went up from the guests, Calvin looked up to find her beside him. "The Yule log is traditionally lit on Christmas Eve," she explained, smiling at him. "You see, Mr. Sharp, as long as the log burns, the slaves are supposed to have holiday." She lowered her voice. "It's said they usually bring in the biggest, most waterlogged log they can find. So it'll burn long." She sighed. "Of course, after New Year's the log is put out. And things go back to normal."

She offered him a sprig of holly from a bunch she held in her left hand.

He took it. "What's this for?"

"You throw it into the fire. And your woes are supposed to go into the fire with it."

He smiled. "A good idea. If only it were that easy."

"We can only do the best we can," she said. "And trust in

God." And with a last smile she moved on, offering holly to the other guests.

Calvin looked at the green sprig in his hand. Throw it into the fire. Get rid of his woes. He'd like to do that. But there was no way to rid himself of his biggest woe—that he was feeling far too much for a Southern belle, a slave-owning Southern belle, who was beyond his reach anyway.

The day before Christmas came to a close, and Calvin made his way to his bedroom and read Willie the Christmas story from the Bible, smiling as he watched the boy search for the letter of the night. Willie was a quick study. Name him a letter once and he knew it. After they got North, Calvin meant to see the boy got proper schooling, learned to read and write and cipher. And when he was old enough, maybe he could even go to university.

Calvin saw Willie settled on his cot and knelt to say his prayers. Then he climbed into bed. Beau and others like him were deceiving themselves, claiming slaves were animals, stupid, brutish. And, all the time, slaves were human beings, just as decent, just as capable as any other people of learning. And as for having good character—why, he'd take Willie as a companion any day over Beau or the colonel or a good many others. *Yes, Lord,* he thought, *it was a good, good day, the day You showed me I should buy Willie. Thank You.*

❧

"Massa! Wake up, Massa! You got to wake up! Please!"

Calvin fought his way up out of deep sleep, out of a beautiful dream in which he and Sarah were walking together under the soft Southern moon, laughing and talking, planning a future together. It couldn't be Christmas morning yet.

Someone was shaking him, shaking him hard. "Wh–what?" he sputtered, opening his eyes. "Willie?" Willie was bending over him. Even in the dim candlelight, it was easy to read the terror on the boy's face. Something was terribly wrong.

Calvin sat up, instantly awake. "What is it? What's wrong?"

"Massa, the paddyrollers." Willie's voice quivered. "The paddyrollers come by."

"Paddyrollers?"

Willie's head bobbed. "Paddyrollers. Looking for runaways or them trying to go north."

Calvin nodded. "But why come by here tonight? It's Christmas Eve."

"Christmas a good time," Willie explained. "Slaves run away then. They don't be missed so soon. Paddyrollers looking for runaway, woman with a li'l baby."

"And—?" Calvin asked. Willie must know something about this runaway. Otherwise he wouldn't be shaking like a leaf.

Willie's chin trembled. "Paregoric all gone. Minta give it to babies, see. Keep 'em from crying. But it all gone. And iffen Vickers come by and the baby cry, Minta—" He gulped and tried again. "Minta be in big trouble. Big, big trouble."

Calvin took Willie by his thin shoulders. "Are you telling me Minta's hiding this runaway? In her cabin?"

Willie nodded, tears running down his cheeks. "Yes, Massa. Minta allus hides 'em."

Always? Minta had done this before? What had he stumbled into? "Where?"

"Got a hole in the floor, dug it under her bed boards where she sleep, covered the boards with corn husks in ticking, like we does. Minta hides 'em under there."

Calvin reached for his trousers. "How do you know the paddyrollers are coming?"

"I's coming back to the big house, coming up the lane. I heard the horses so I stepped offen the path. Then I seen the paddyrollers, heading for Vickers's cabin." He hesitated, straightening his shoulders. "And I know 'bout the runaway 'cause I was at Minta's. I–I help her."

"I see," Calvin said, keeping his voice calm. The boy was scared enough as it was. Calvin pulled on his boots and reached for his shirt. "You've helped Minta before, then?"

Willie gulped again, but he answered bravely enough, "Yes, Massa. When I live here, I help Miss Sarah and—"

Calvin shot to his feet, his heart about to leap out through his open mouth. "Sarah!" He lowered his voice. "Sarah's part of this?"

Willie had retreated a step, but now he nodded vigorously. "Yes, Massa. Her and her mama. Only tonight Missus too sick to help."

Calvin grabbed his coat. "What will Vickers do? Will he take the paddyrollers to Slave Row?"

Willie shook his head. "No, Massa. Paddyrollers go on, tell others. Vickers, he make all the slaves get out their cabins. He don't care what time it is. He go through all them cabins. And iffen that baby cry—"

"In my bag," Calvin said, a desperate plan forming in his mind. "Get the bottle of whiskey in my bag." He'd kept the bottle for purely medicinal purposes and had never expected to have this sort of use for it.

"Yes, Massa." Willie hurried over and pulled out the bottle. "Here it is."

"Now," Calvin said. "As soon as the paddyrollers are gone, I'll find Vickers."

"They be gone now, Massa. They gives the news and rides on to the next place."

Calvin waved the bottle. "I'll offer Vickers the bottle." He squeezed Willie's shoulder. "Don't be upset by the way I behave. I won't really be drunk. I won't be drinking at all."

Willie nodded, his eyes big.

"Just stay in the shadows 'til I come for you."

Willie managed a weak grin. "Yes, Massa; I wait. I knowed you could fix it."

Calvin wasn't all that sure, but he meant to do what he could. He wasn't going to let Sarah come to harm if he could help it. "Let's get going."

Stepping softly, he followed Willie out the hall and down the stairs. The house was dark and quiet, everyone sleeping after the pre-Christmas revelry. As they crept down the stairs, Calvin sent up a silent prayer that the Gordons would keep on sleeping. He didn't need Beau or his father coming out to mess this up. Or the colonel either, for that matter.

Calvin hurried across the moonlit yard with Willie, slipping from shadow to shadow 'til they reached an outbuilding about twenty feet from Vickers's cabin.

Willie stopped. "I be praying, Massa," he whispered. "I be praying real hard."

"Me too. Real hard." Calvin pulled his coat awry and staggered toward Vickers's cabin, singing a drunken song. He was almost there when the door burst open and Vickers came barreling out, stuffing his shirt into his trousers. "What the—"

" 'Lo, there," Calvin cried jovially, throwing an arm

around Vickers's shoulders. "Wanna drink?"

Vickers peered at him from his bleary eyes. "Drink? Whishkey?"

"The best," Calvin mumbled and handed the bottle over. The man was already two sheets to the wind. If only this worked. *Please God. Make it work. It's got to work.*

While they stumbled on, Calvin's thoughts raced. He could hardly believe that Sarah was helping runaways. He didn't know whether to be happy about what she was doing or scared half to death. He *was* happy, happy to know that Sarah wasn't just a Southern belle whose soft feelings were reserved for her personal slaves. She was a God-fearing woman, ready to stand up for her beliefs. He just hoped they didn't get her in trouble. *O God, keep her safe. Please keep her safe.*

Vickers stumbled against him, lurching heavily, and at the same time raised the bottle and took a big swig. When he didn't pass the bottle back, Calvin reached for it. After all, he was supposed to be drunk.

It took some struggle to wrest the bottle from Vickers, and when Calvin did, he only pretended to drink. He certainly didn't mean to put his lips anywhere near where Vickers's had been. The very thought made him ill. The man stank, probably hadn't had a bath in days. His clothes smelled of stale whiskey and vomit and sweat—a horrible odor. And his breath wasn't much better.

Calvin angled toward a big oak in the yard, passing the bottle back to Vickers as they went. "Good whishkey," Vickers mumbled. "Real good."

They reached the oak and Calvin tumbled down on the grass at its foot and broke out laughing. Vickers fell too. Slumped there on the grass, they passed the bottle back and forth between them. Calvin didn't drink, of course. He carried whiskey only for medicinal purposes—snakebite and things like that. He didn't touch alcohol. Never had. As a seven-year-old, he'd made that promise to his grieving mother the day they laid his father in his grave. And he'd never broken it. He never would. He might be the son of a drunkard, but he didn't intend to become a drunkard himself.

But now he wished he'd carried more than one bottle. What if one wasn't enough? What if Vickers got up from the grass and reeled off toward Slave Row? What if he heard that baby cry? *Please, God, no,* Calvin prayed. *Make the whiskey do its work. Help me keep Sarah safe. And Minta and the others. Please.*

The bottle passed back and forth, getting emptier and emptier. And Vickers appeared to be unaffected. As the level of whiskey sank, Calvin's spirits sank with it. Would the man never pass out?

Finally, when he'd about given up hope, a strange sound issued from Vickers. Calvin held his breath. *Was that—? Could it be—?* The sound came again. *A snore!* Vickers was snoring!

Thank You, God! Thank You.

Slowly, carefully, Calvin eased himself away. Holding his breath, he got to his feet and took one step, then another. Vickers didn't move. Calvin left him there, the empty bottle clutched in his hand, snores issuing from his lips, and started back toward the house. But he'd only gone a few feet when Willie appeared beside him and wrapped his arms around his leg in a great hug.

"I knowed you could do it, Massa! Praise Jesus!"

Calvin pried the boy loose. "Praise Him, indeed," he

whispered. "Now take me to Minta's cabin. We've got to get them out of there before he wakes up."

Willie didn't hesitate, but set off across the grass, Calvin right behind him.

eight

Sarah paced the dirt floor of Minta's cabin, ten steps one way, six steps the other. While she paced, she hummed a lullaby to the tiny baby cradled in her arms. He was hungry, poor little thing. Probably cold, too, with nothing but an old flour sack wrapped around him. What a time to run out of paregoric. She should have been more careful, but she had so much on her mind, with Mama being sick and all the company coming and trying to keep from being left alone with Beau and with Mr. Sharp being there. Truth was, she'd just plain forgotten.

She held the baby close against her chest, trying to warm him with heat from her own body and the corners of her shawl that she'd pulled over him. She would like to wrap him completely in her shawl, to leave it on him. But if the patrollers caught the runaway, that shawl could be recognized. Papa had sent away for it, all the way to Paris, and if it went missing, he'd want to know what had happened to it. So she couldn't send it with the woman.

She looked down at the baby. There was only a tiny fire on the hearth, but she could see his little face in the moonlight shining through the paneless windows. He peered up at her from big dark eyes. What was he thinking—if babies *could* think? Was he wondering why he was so cold and hungry? Was he wishing he was back with God and His angels?

"Miss Sarah," Minta said, putting a hand on her shoulder.

"We got to hide the baby now." She cast a worried glance at the door. "Paddyrollers could be coming. Ole Vickers, too, maybe."

Sarah looked toward the sleeping corner where the corn-husk mattress and boards had been pushed aside and the exhausted slave woman lay shivering in the hidey-hole lined with rags, her torn dress and bloody feet mute testi-mony to how far she'd traveled. There was barely room to move in that hole, not enough to lie out straight, so she had to curl up. But it was the only place they had to hide her.

"She jest too wore out to go on," Minta said, shaking her head. "Got to rest a day or so. Maybe more."

Sarah sighed. "If only we had a wagon. Or a carriage."

Minta shook her head. "There be a reward out by now, I guess. Paddyrollers looking hard. They don't let no wag-ons or carriages through without searching 'em. She safer here."

Minta took the baby from Sarah and eased him down into his mother's waiting arms. The woman managed a lit-tle smile and nestled the baby to her breast. "Lord Jesus bless you," she murmured.

"You don't worry," Minta said. "We pass lotsa slaves through here." She covered the woman with a tattered quilt. From her own bed, Sarah knew. "This keep you warm," Minta said. "I cover the hole now. Don't be scared."

Sarah helped Minta replace the boards and arrange the cornhusk mattress over them again, then stood back to make sure it looked normal. Minta frowned. "You shouldna come down here this late, Miss Sarah."

Sarah shrugged. "I told Willie to let me know if any run-aways came in. I wanted at least to bring out some bread and cheese. I can't take much more tonight without it being missed. But at least I could bring that. The woman has to eat if she's going to feed the baby."

"But if Massa find out—"

"He won't," Sarah said, but she couldn't quite hold back a shiver. "But even if he does, I have to do what I can. Slavery is wrong. So wrong. People shouldn't own other people."

Minta nodded. "I knows that, Miss Sarah. It do make a great heaviness on a person's mind, being a slave. But I used to it."

"Oh, Minta, if only I could do something else! If I could free you."

Minta shook her head. "You can't—an' that's that. But I lucky. I knows you got a good heart. Ain't many Southern folk like you, Miss Sarah. Not many." Her head came up. "Hist! Someone a-comin'. What you gonna tell 'em?"

Sarah's heart pounded and her hands went clammy, but she wouldn't panic. She just wouldn't. She'd prepared for this possibility many times. "Mama. I'll tell them Mama was sick and I came for you."

Footsteps drew nearer to the door, and she faced it, trying not to look as frightened as she felt. The door swung open. Her heart rose up in her throat—and hung there, beating wildly.

"Mr. Sharp!" Of all the people she'd imagined opening that door, he was the last. "What are *you* doing here?"

"I think that's my question," he said softly, motioning to Willie to close the door behind him.

"I—" she stammered. "Mama was sick. I came to get Minta."

He looked around the cabin, his dark gaze probing every shadowy corner. Was it her imagination, or did he look longer at the corner with its cornhusk bed? But he couldn't know about the hidey-hole.

"It all right, Miss Sarah," Willie said, coming to tug at her hand. "Massa, he know."

Surely Willie didn't mean— "Knows what?" she made herself ask.

"Willie's trying to tell you that I'm on your side," Mr. Sharp said, his voice gentle. "That I'm here to help."

She wanted to believe him. With all her heart and soul she wanted to believe him. But she couldn't risk that poor woman and her baby being dragged away, back to slavery. "I don't know what you're talking about."

"Minta," Willie said, running to his sister. "Tell Miss Sarah that Massa want to help."

Minta bent to hug him. "Hush, chil'. Miss Sarah thinkin'."

"But, Minta," Willie insisted, "Massa keep ole Vickers from coming here."

Minta straightened. "He what?"

"Massa, he take his whiskey bottle." Willie grinned. "He get ole Vickers so drunk, he pass out. He laying out there under a big oak. Right now."

Sarah's heart pounded in her chest. Mr. Sharp had helped them! She felt relief wash over her, blessed relief that there was someone *to* help. She took the few steps that put her close enough to take his hands in her own. "Why, Mr. Sharp? Why did you do that?"

"Willie woke me up," he said, his dear face so serious in the moonlight coming through the window. It *was* dear to her; she knew that now. "He told me the paddyrollers were waking Vickers," he went on, "and that he'd soon be searching the cabins. Willie was worried about you and Minta, because you're out of paregoric, he said, and if the baby cried, you could all be in big trouble."

"I tol' you, Miss Sarah," Willie said, his bright eyes looking on Mr. Sharp with pride. "Massa the bestest man ever. He believe in Lord Jesus, too. He read me good stories from the Bible—every night. An' we pray."

Sarah looked down. She was still holding Mr. Sharp's hands, but she didn't want to let them go. There was strength in his hands, strength and comfort. And a feeling of rightness—how strange—a feeling of coming home. "Mr. Sharp, you did this for us?"

He nodded. "I don't believe in slavery. It's morally wrong." He glanced at the bed corner again. "The danger is averted for the moment, but we've got to get them out of here. Vickers will wake up, you know."

Sarah shook her head. "She can't go on tonight. She can hardly walk. Her feet are all bloody. And it's less than a week since she's had the baby. If only we had a wagon— or a carriage."

"Can she sit a horse?" he asked.

Sarah straightened. "I don't know. Can she, Minta?"

Minta frowned. "Guess she could iffen she was riding double, had someone to hold onto her so she don't slip off. Suppose we could tie the baby to her chest with some rags. But the paddyrollers got bloodhounds sometimes. If they—"

Mr. Sharp smiled slightly. "I don't think they can follow her if she's off the ground." He turned to Sarah. "You know, since Willie came into my care, I've become very interested in following the North Star. Willie told me something about this mysterious Underground Railroad." He grinned. "You see, I took pains to learn about ways to get slaves north to freedom."

Sarah gripped his hands tighter. Had he taken those pains because of *her?*

"Maybe I can get your runaway to the next station and be back here before daylight. If Willie knows the way."

"I does!" Willie cried. "We can do it."

"This is very dangerous," Sarah said, her heart full to overflowing. "There's a thousand-dollar fine for helping runaways. And six months in prison, at the very least. It could be a lot more."

"We ain't gonna get caught," Willie said, his eyes gleaming with excitement. "We Pinkerton men. 'Sides, I been there before. I know the way. I be sure we don't get caught."

Minta nodded. "Willie good in the woods. Real good."

Mr. Sharp nodded. "I know. Someday I'll tell you how he helped me catch a counterfeiter. But now, you'd better get the woman ready to go."

"I do it," Minta said, looking from Sarah to Mr. Sharp. "Willie, you go get them horses."

Sarah moved to disengage her hands from Mr. Sharp's, to help Minta ready the woman, but something in his look stopped her. "Mr. Sharp?"

"Call me Calvin," he said. "Please."

Why did her heart pound so? She'd been wanting to use his Christian name, wanting it almost from the day she'd met him. "Calvin. Please let go of my hands."

He squeezed them instead. "In a moment. I just have a question to ask you."

"I will answer it if I can," she said.

His gaze held hers. "How will you do this kind of thing when you have become Mrs. Beauregard Gordon? I can't imagine that he would approve of such behavior."

A shiver slithered over her. "No, he wouldn't. But I don't want to marry Beau. I don't like him very much." Goodness, what had she said to make Calvin smile that happily?

"You mean that?" he asked. "You really don't want to marry him?"

"Of course I mean it. Papa wants us to marry soon, but we keep putting him off—Mama and me."

He came a step closer. "Miss Hawthorne—"

"Sarah," she breathed, wondering at her own forwardness. "Please call me Sarah."

"Sarah," he said, and her name on his lips was so sweet, it made her feel all warm inside.

"I know we've only been acquainted a short time," he went on, his dark face serious, "but you must have been aware of my regard, of my tender feelings for you."

"I—" The look in his eyes was tender—and, yes, so were her feelings for him. Very tender. She nodded.

His face grew even more serious. "I would go to your father and ask his permission to court—"

"No!" she cried. "I mean, you mustn't do that. Papa would only say no. And—and he might make you leave."

"And you don't want that?" he asked, his eyes warm, his smile returning.

Where was her maidenly modesty? She shouldn't be speaking to him like this. But they had so little time. And she cared about him so much. "I don't want you to go."

"Then will you keep putting Beau off? Will you give me hope that someday, someway, I might come back to claim you as my wife?"

She didn't even hesitate. She knew her own heart. "Yes, Calvin. I will wait for you. I won't let Papa make me marry Beau. Not now. I just won't."

"Good." Calvin drew her into his arms for a brief hug. How strong and warm he was. How safe she felt there, how at home. And he didn't even try to kiss her. He wasn't at all like Beau.

"Now you get back to the Big House," he said. "And rest well. I'll see you at breakfast."

"God speed you," she whispered against his shoulder. "And bring you safely back to me."

"He will," Calvin said, releasing her. "After all, I am going about His work."

"She be ready now," Minta said.

Sarah turned. While they'd stood there talking as though there was no one in the world but them, Minta had moved the cornhusk mattress and boards and gotten the woman out of the hole. She stood there, leaning on Minta's shoulder, the baby tied to her chest, a small woman, very thin, her dress in tatters. Calvin took one look at her and shrugged out of his coat. He put it around her shoulders and buttoned it below the baby.

Then he picked her up in his arms. "Get the door," he told Minta. "And then see that Sarah gets to bed."

"Yes, Massa," Minta said, grinning. "I do that for sure."

Sarah watched him go, the brave, good man she loved. And he loved her, too. She could hardly believe it.

"I told you he a good man," Minta said, dropping to her knees in the dirt. "Lord Jesus, keep 'em all safe. Please. And bring Mr. Calvin and Willie right back."

Sarah sank to her knees too, tears of happiness rising to her eyes. "And thank You, God. Thank You for sending Calvin to help that poor woman and her baby. Amen."

nine

On Christmas morning, Calvin left his bedchamber and
started down to breakfast, his face wreathed in a big smile.
He'd been wakened by Willie crying, "Christmas gif',"
and had given him a shiny coin and the whispered promise
of schooling when they returned North. Then he'd sent
Willie down to the kitchen so he could participate in the
holiday festivities there, and under the cloak of them
deliver to Minta the bottle of paregoric they'd brought
back from the Underground station. He wanted no more
emergencies in Minta's cabin.

Calvin smoothed his waistcoat and tried not to smile so
broadly. Though he'd been up most of the night, and spent
a lot of it on horseback, he wasn't the least bit tired. He had
a lot of faith in this mysterious Underground Railroad of
the abolitionists. He felt in his bones that the runaway and
her child would make it safe to Canada, to freedom and the
husband she'd told him waited for her there. The joy of
rescuing them had made him feel that he'd really been
walking with God, really doing something worthwhile and
important. And what an appropriate night for it, the night
when another Baby had been born to set men free.

"Praise Jesus!" Willie had whispered after they'd sneaked
past the still-snoring Vickers and back into the dark house
to reach their room. And Calvin's thanksgiving, though
silent, had been equally joyous.

Now in the morning light he made his way down the

stairs, secure in the knowledge that today nothing Beauregard Gordon or his father, or any other guest, could say could dim the joy in Calvin Sharp's heart. Because of a midnight ride, two human beings had been set free, free as they were meant to be. That tiny baby would never know the chains of slavery, would never be beaten. That was a fine thing to think about on this holy day. Now he could understand in a way he never had before why men risked their own lives, their own freedom, to secure that of others.

He should be trying to look a little less joyful, though. He couldn't go around grinning all the time. People might get to wondering why he looked so happy. But he was supremely happy—because of last night, and because in his heart he carried the marvelous knowledge that Sarah really cared about him, that she didn't want him to leave Hawthorne Hill. Anxiety hit him for a second, though. Was she really strong enough to resist the colonel? Maybe not on her own. But she had her mother to help her. And God. They would have to trust in God. That was what Mother had taught him. "Do all that you can, Son," she had said. "And then trust in God." Calvin resumed walking. Trust in God; that was what he'd always done.

The dining room was crowded, chattering guests clustered around the sideboard loaded with food. Pausing there, Calvin saw the food laid out, a finely sliced ham, eggs, spoon bread and egg bread and another bread full of raisins, eggs, oysters, fresh fish, fruit, and cheese. And a silver pot of coffee, cups stacked beside it. But he wasn't really interested in food. Not this morning, not with his heart bursting with joy.

He searched for Sarah. And there she was—across the room, with her back to him. But he would recognize her anywhere, the dark hair and the shape and size of her. He started toward her, eager just to be close to her. And then she turned. In that second he saw joy on her face, in her eyes. Joy at seeing *him*. But it was only there for that second. Then her eyes clouded over, and her gaze moved away, beyond him.

"Good morning, my dear," Beau said from behind him. "You're looking lovely this morning. As always." He passed Calvin and went to raise Sarah's hand to his lips.

"Thank you," Sarah said, leaving her hand in his for a moment. But there was no joy in her face now. Calvin took heart at that. Sarah might have to pretend, because of the colonel, that Beau was agreeable to her, but she wasn't going to let her father marry her to the man. She had promised to wait until she could become Mrs. Calvin Sharp. Calvin didn't know *how* he would manage it, but he would. He wanted Sarah to be his wife. Surely God had led him to the auction house on purpose, to Willie, and to Sarah—the only woman he'd ever loved. Surely God would show him how they could be together.

"Help yourself, Mr. Sharp." Mrs. Hawthorne had come to stand beside him, somewhat obscuring his view of Sarah in her holiday gown. "We're glad to have you here for the holidays."

Something in her gaze gave him warning, and he turned away from watching Sarah and Beau, and managed a smile.

"Thank you, ma'am. I've really enjoyed it."

Mrs. Hawthorne nodded. "That's good. Perhaps you'll join us tonight for Minta's wedding. She's marrying Hiram, the colonel's head driver. There'll be much music and dancing in the slave quarters. A great feast." She smiled. "We wanted to make Minta's wedding a fine time. She's a favorite of ours."

Calvin nodded. *Hiram?* Wasn't that the driver that Vickers had mentioned to the colonel, the one who'd given the lash to the so-called lazy slave? How could Sarah's mother approve of Minta marrying a traitor to her people, someone who beat his fellow slaves? How would Minta help runaways if she married such a man? But one thing he'd learned through life—people were not always what they seemed. Mrs. Hawthorne, Sarah, Minta, Willie, to say nothing of himself, were all wearing false faces. No reason this Hiram couldn't too.

"Thank you," Calvin said, smiling at his hostess, "for inviting me. I'd enjoy seeing that."

"Then we'll consider that you'll escort us," she said, giving him a glance that made him wonder how much she knew of the feelings of his heart. "I expect all our guests will be going."

Calvin filled his plate and took a place at the table, a place where he could see Sarah. Beau sat beside her, of course, after he had filled a plate for her and one for himself and leaned toward her as though no one else were in the room.

"So, Mr. Sharp," the colonel said, nodding in his direction. "How do you find our fair South?"

"It's beautiful country," Calvin said. Better to stick to the scenery. No use talking to these people about the injustice of slavery. They wouldn't hear him anyway. Their minds were set.

"Yes, it is," the colonel said. "A beautiful country. And all built upon an institution of divine appointment."

Divine appointment? Calvin struggled to keep his expression blank. Did the man really think that God meant for whole races of people to be enslaved?

"Yes," the colonel went on complacently. "The Lord designed it so well. The slaves benefit as much as we do, you see," he continued. "I just wish the Northerners would understand that."

This time Calvin had a real struggle to keep his feelings from showing on his face. Benefit? That poor creature who'd cut her feet to the bone to carry her newborn child to freedom—she surely didn't think slavery was a benefit.

"You're so right," Mr. Gordon said, wiping his greasy mouth on an even greasier napkin. "This demon democracy the Northerners keep spouting off about—" He cast Calvin a sharp glance. "My apologies, Mr. Sharp. But I'm only speaking the truth."

Calvin nodded. It was the most he could do. He was afraid to open his mouth. If he did, he might not be able to control what came out of it.

"Yes," the colonel said, nodding his patrician head. "The nonsensical prating of abolitionists about abstract notions of human rights completely ignores the fact that slavery is good for all of us. The slaves need us as much as we need them. We are lifting them out of their barbarism, helping them to become civilized."

Heads nodded around the table, women's as well as men's. Sarah nodded, too, carefully avoiding Calvin's glance. She had to agree, he supposed, to keep the peace with her father. If she didn't, she'd be unable to continue helping runaways. It was a bad position for her to be in, though, having to live a lie. He supposed she was doing the best she could. But how he longed to get up on the two good feet God had given him and tell these people what a terrible offense they were committing, an offense against God Himself. He kept his counsel, though, kept his face straight, and his fisted hands under the table where they couldn't be seen.

"Today being Christmas," Mrs. Hawthorne said, turning to speak to him, "we will give each woman several lengths of cloth, and two handkerchiefs for her head. The men will each get a shirt and a good pair of woolen trousers and the little ones each a new shirt of homespun. And hard candy, of course. They do so love that candy."

Mrs. Gordon nodded. "Yes," she said softly, the first word he'd ever heard her utter. "Before we left, we—"

"Well, Colonel," Beau said, cutting his mother off as though she didn't exist. "How soon can we sample that famous eggnog of yours?"

A look of disgust crossed Sarah's face and was gone. She put a forkful of ham in her mouth.

The colonel chuckled. "Right now, Beau. The eggnog's coming right now." He motioned to the butler. "Albert, it's time to bring out the eggnog."

"Yes, Master. Right away."

Albert returned with a silver tray holding a tall silver pitcher, glass goblets, and a nest of silver spoons. With great ceremony, he set the tray before the colonel. "No milk in it?" the colonel inquired.

Albert made a face of exasperated horror. "No milk in our eggnog, Master. We make it the Georgia way. Cook uses well-beaten eggs, sugar, and brandy, mixed with rum. We wouldn't dilute it with milk."

"Very good." The colonel smiled and lifted the pitcher. "I'm sure you'll all enjoy it."

Calvin stiffened in his chair. Alcohol with breakfast yet.

No wonder these people behaved as they did. Well, now he had another problem. What should he do? He could plead the Pinkerton Agency rule against operatives drinking, but these people might not believe him. They were obviously used to indulging themselves. And besides, what if Vickers had said something to the colonel about the drinking with Calvin last night? What if the colonel suspected Calvin had had something to do with Vickers passing out under the oak? But surely Vickers would keep quiet about his own drunkenness. The colonel and Beau had just been talking about renewing overseers' contracts, saying it would soon be time. So Vickers wouldn't want to look bad. He wouldn't want to jeopardize his position.

Calvin's thoughts raced in circles. He didn't want to put Minta and Sarah in danger. There was need for the work they were doing, great need, and he would do all he could to protect them. But, at the same time, there was nothing on the face of this earth that would make him break his word to his sainted mother.

The colonel filled the crystal goblets one by one and passed them down the table. Calvin straightened his shoulders. He'd have to speak up, and he might as well do it now. "I'm afraid I'll have to forego the eggnog, Colonel. I'm sorry."

Everyone at the table turned to look at him as though he'd suddenly said the moon was made of green cheese. Or that slaves were human beings.

"I insist," the colonel said. "It's really more palatable than it sounds."

Calvin shook his head. "It's not that, sir. It sounds delicious." Well, surely he was allowed a little leeway. He couldn't afford to insult the man. "It's just that Mr. Pinkerton has very strict regulations for his operatives. And not drinking spirits is one of them." He'd better qualify that, in case Vickers did talk. Calvin looked the colonel straight in the eye. "Mr. Pinkerton is my employer and as a man of honor I do my best to follow his regulations."

"Of course," the colonel said, but his eyes were steely. *Had* he been talking to Vickers? There was no way to tell. Besides, Calvin had other things to be thinking about.

Across the table, Beau was passing a goblet to Sarah, his eyes warm, his fingers touching hers. "To us, my dear," he said, smiling at her and raising his own goblet. "And to our early marriage."

Calvin stiffened, then forced himself to relax. At least he didn't have to drink to that. The thought of such a marriage made his blood run cold.

Sarah raised her goblet to her lips. She could hardly do otherwise with Beau and her father watching her. But the goblet looked just as full when she set it down as it had when she picked it up.

Beau didn't seem to notice. "Too bad," he said, giving Calvin a patronizing look, "that Mr. Pinkerton treats his operatives like a bunch of babies. A good drink never hurt a *man*."

That was one of the biggest lies in the world, but Calvin didn't intend to dispute it. He wasn't going to resurrect the memory of his drunken father dying in the middle of a muddy street, run over by a wagon because he was too befuddled to get out of the way. These people wouldn't learn anything from it.

But since everyone was waiting for him to say something, Calvin managed a smile. "Mr. Pinkerton has his reasons, I'm sure. An operative sometimes works in dangerous places. A man whose thoughts are centered on his next bottle, or even his next pipe, is not a man prepared to give his all to the job."

Beau shrugged his elegantly clothed shoulders. "I shouldn't like to work for your Mr. Pinkerton. Being an operative doesn't sound like much fun."

Calvin struggled to keep his expression friendly. What a fool this Beau was, a pampered spoiled fool. *Sorry, Lord, but he is.* And to think that Sarah's father would give her in marriage to him just like that, because he was a so-called Southern gentleman. "Most work is not much fun," Calvin said dryly, "but most work still has to be done."

"Speaking of work," Mrs. Hawthorne intervened, smiling at her guests. "I believe it's time for us ladies to leave you. I have a lot to do to see that our dinner is properly prepared. And don't forget that there'll be music and dancing in the quarters tonight. Since this is his first Christmas in the South, I've invited Mr. Sharp to come along and see what a slave wedding is like." She got to her feet and the other women followed suit. "We'll see you all later."

The day passed slowly. And no matter what Calvin did, he couldn't manage to say more than a couple words to Sarah before Beau was there, beaming down on her and crowding him out. And given the circumstances, he couldn't do much about it.

Finally, near three o'clock, the Christmas dinner was put on the table. Staring at the profusion of food—turkey, potatoes, stuffing, gravy, pickled mangoes, brandied peaches, ham, roast beef, oysters, vegetables swimming in butter or with egg or in other sauces—Calvin sighed. How could these people keep stuffing themselves?

He'd grown up on scant rations, and he still ate sparingly, partly from habit and partly because he saw no sense in being a glutton.

He took one helping of everything, but the other men apparently felt no need to be careful. Mr. Gordon took seconds, then thirds, and finally fourths, leaving liberal traces of his meal on his bulging waistcoat. Beau also ate heartily, but Mrs. Gordon pushed the food around on her plate, hardly eating anything, and avoiding her husband's gaze. Of the others, the men ate heartily, and the women more sparingly. Sarah didn't seem to be eating a great deal, but perhaps that was her usual way. Or perhaps, like him, she was too full of happiness to give much thought to food. He liked that thought.

Calvin finished with a slice of the plum pudding which Mrs. Hawthorne had announced was the pièce de résistance of the day, carried in, flaming, by a servant, after a meal that took over two hours. Calvin thought about the people around him, how different they were from the ones he'd known all his life. They looked like other people; they ate and drank, but they spoke about slaves as though they were dogs, or less, as though some of those same slaves weren't right there serving the food on their plates and hearing what was said about them. Did Southerners really think slaves couldn't hear, couldn't understand? And how could Southerners believe they had the right to enslave others? He found it very hard to understand. Hard? Impossible was more like it!

ten

Upstairs, after dinner, Sarah slipped off her shoes and lay back on her bed. She wiggled her toes, stretched, and closed her eyes. She hadn't slept much last night. She hadn't been worried about Mr. Sharp and Willie being caught by the patrollers. At least, she hadn't been worried a lot. Calvin— she repeated his name silently and with a sense of joy— Calvin knew how to take care of himself. What had kept her awake last night was the memory, the precious memory, of the words she and Calvin had exchanged, the promises they'd made to each other.

It might seem silly to some people that she'd promised to wait for him, to marry him someday, a man she'd only known for a few days. But it didn't seem silly to her. She'd watched him closely, that day at the auction hall when he bought Willie and these days that he'd been a guest at the Hill. What she'd seen had made her sure that he was a good man, a trustworthy man. And what he'd done last night—risking his own safety like that for some- one he didn't even know, that was a marvelous Christian thing. He was the man God intended for her. She knew it in her heart.

She smiled. Now she understood much better why Minta wanted to marry Hiram, why she wanted to spend her life with him, if she could. That wonderful feeling of belong- ing to someone was impossible to describe. She would never have imagined she could feel like this. So—special.

The day was passing slowly, more slowly even after Mama had told her she'd asked Mr. Sharp to escort them to the quarters after supper tonight to watch the slave dancing. Sarah smiled. She was looking forward to being with Calvin and Mama. But in the meantime, there had been Beau to contend with. He'd kept trying to get her under the mistletoe for another kiss, which she'd managed to avoid, though only with a good deal of effort. And at breakfast he had been so rude to Calvin, with his nasty remarks about men who didn't drink. As though drinking like a fish and eating like a pig and treating your wife like dirt were manly things to do!

Calvin knew how to be a man. He didn't have to bully people. Look at Willie. Willie had always been a frightened, shy little boy, hardly able to speak to anyone but her and Minta. And now, in two short months with Calvin, Willie had blossomed into a child with bright eyes and a chance at a future. Oh, yes, Calvin was a wonderful man. A man of God, and she meant to marry him somehow, someway.

Please, Lord, she prayed. *You sent him to me. Please show me how we can be together. And thank You. Amen.*

When they left the Big House for Slave Row after supper that night, strolling down a path between rows of blazing torches, Calvin had Mrs. Hawthorne on one arm and Sarah on the other. Mrs. Hawthorne had arranged it with a look at Beau that had made him back off, a look that had given Calvin cause to reconsider his opinion of her as a frail Southern matron. She might be ailing, but Sarah's mother had a will of iron. Of course, considering what she'd been doing behind her husband's back all these years, Calvin might have expected that.

But looks could be deceiving. Look at the pale and invisible Mrs. Gordon, a nonentity if he'd ever seen one. But who knew what she was doing when no one was around to see? He almost laughed aloud. He was definitely letting his imagination run away with him if he started giving a secret life to Mrs. Gordon!

He turned his attention back to Sarah. "Are there festivities like this in the quarters every Christmas?" he asked.

She nodded. In the light of the torches, her face glowed with pleasure. He hoped it was pleasure at being with him. He knew how good he felt being with her.

"Yes," she said. "Christmas is a big time in the quarters. I told you about the Yule log. We always provide a big feast, too, a barbecue and other good things to eat."

She smiled at him. "And tonight is even more special, because Minta and Hiram are getting married."

"How is that done?" Calvin asked. Conscious that Beau was pacing behind them, and almost able to feel the man's animosity burning into the back of his neck, Calvin turned this question to Mrs. Hawthorne. "Do you have a preacher here on the plantation or do you bring one in?"

Mrs. Hawthorne shook her head. "Neither, Mr. Sharp. The colonel holds that slaves don't need such niceties. And, of course, I agree with him."

She didn't, he knew. But there wasn't a hint of sarcasm or indignation in her voice—only her eyes gave her away. Violet eyes like Sarah's, they told him her pain at being part of this injustice, her anger at her husband for his participation in it.

From behind them Beau snorted. "Nigras don't need no preacher. Marriage don't mean anything to them."

Calvin felt Sarah's arm stiffen, but she remained silent.

He paused and half turned to meet Beau's gaze. "You'll have to excuse me, Mr. Gordon. I'm woefully ignorant of Southern customs. And in my ignorance I assumed that all creatures capable of speech were capable of making promises to each other. But it seems I was wrong."

Beau bristled and seemed to know he'd been insulted, but the words, and even the tone, had been innocuous enough. And even Beau knew better than to push things in front of Sarah and her mother. "If you lived down here, you'd understand in a hurry," he contented himself with muttering.

If I lived down here, Calvin thought bitterly, *things would be a lot different.* But he refused to be drawn further into discussion. Besides, as they neared the quarters the music increased in volume, making much conversation difficult. He made out the sound of a fiddle and drums, and perhaps other instruments. He couldn't be sure.

The slaves had gathered around a great square of beaten earth. To one side a huge bonfire roared skyward. Opposite it, blazing torches were stuck in the ground. On the far side of the square from the visitors stood a trestle laden with food. And nearest them was a row of chairs, obviously designated for white spectators since no slaves were anywhere close by them.

In the center of the square, brightly dressed dancers stomped and whirled to the fastest music he'd ever heard. He'd never seen such gyrations before, but the general good humor and joy were plain. There went Minta, wearing a new calico gown, a wreath of greens in her hair, her bare feet pounding and twirling as she swung around with a big burly man. Hiram, no doubt. Well, if Minta loved him and Sarah approved the match, there must be more to the man than met the eye. And from the way he looked at Minta, and the way Minta looked back, the two were much in love.

Calvin frowned. How on earth could Beau believe that slaves were incapable of fidelity, of love? But then, what could be expected of a man raised in such a pernicious atmosphere? A man who treated his own mother like a slave? Calvin gave silent thanks for the Christian mother who had raised him to be a decent man, who had taught him that all people belong to God.

"I've had some chairs brought down," Mrs. Hawthorne said, gesturing toward them. "We can sit there to watch the dancing." She looked up at the night sky and drew her shawl closer. "If the weather had turned bad, they would have cleaned out a room in the infirmary and held the dance there."

Calvin had seen the infirmary, where sick slaves lay huddled on the dirt floor under heaps of filthy rags. He hoped never to set foot in such a place again. He pushed the thought out of his mind. This was a time for celebration.

Mrs. Hawthorne settled in a chair. "Sit here between us," she said, gathering her shawl closer. Calvin gave her a grateful glance and turned to help Sarah. The smile she gave him warmed him to the heart. But then Beau took the chair on her other side and leaned toward her, putting a proprietary hand on her arm. Sarah eased her arm away, slowly, as though to rearrange her shawl.

"Is that Hiram that Minta is dancing with?" Calvin asked.

"Yes," Sarah said, leaning closer. Her hand brushed his coat sleeve, but he dared not look down. Her body screened her hand from Beau's sight, but still Calvin had to be careful.

"Do the dances have names?" he asked, for want of

something else to say. "They look quite interesting."

"Yes," Sarah said. "There's one called 'The Chicken Wing.' "

"Names," Beau snorted. "These are savages. Barbarians. They don't bother with names for things."

Calvin held his peace. He wasn't going to let Beau get to him. Not today.

"Look," Mrs. Hawthorne said. "There's Willie."

Calvin looked. And looked again. He'd never have recognized his sobersided Willie in that barefoot whirling dervish cavorting in front of the bonfire. Evidently, the cherished boots had been left up in the bedroom. Probably they didn't work well for dancing.

"I hope you'll be able to stay through New Year's Day, Mr. Sharp," Mrs. Hawthorne said. "We've much enjoyed your company."

Calvin heard the soft intake of Sarah's breath as she waited for his answer. He wished he could give her a better one. "I'm sorry, Mrs. Hawthorne, but I'm afraid I'll have to leave tomorrow. I've got to get back to Chicago. No doubt when I get there, Mr. Pinkerton will have another case waiting for me."

"Oh, that's too bad." Mrs. Hawthorne's gaze held his, and her eyes showed real regret. "Perhaps you'll be able to visit us again sometime."

Calvin didn't turn to look at Sarah. He didn't dare let her see his pain at leaving her, not here where Beau might glimpse it. "Yes, ma'am," he said. "I'd like to do that. I've enjoyed this visit very much. And who knows—perhaps Mr. Pinkerton will send me this way again."

Another soft-drawn breath came from Sarah, and her hand brushed his sleeve again, but all she said was, "Look!

Doesn't Minta look happy?"

"Yes," Calvin said, daring to glance at Sarah for a second before he looked at the dancers. "She looks very happy. She must be much in love."

Sarah nodded, her eyes shining. "Yes, I—"

Beau snorted again. "Love, you say? Nigras don't know nothing about love. How could they, ignorant savages that they are? Really, Mr. Sharp, you *are* woefully ignorant in Southern ways."

"Yes," Calvin said, keeping the anger out of his voice with great effort. "But I am learning." He focused his gaze on the dancing, but in his heart he was praying. *Oh, yes, Lord, I am learning. I am learning to hate the institution of slavery with such passion that I will do everything I can to destroy it, lock, stock, and barrel. This is my solemn vow to You, O Lord, as solemn as the vow I took on my father's grave. I will work to end slavery—as long as I live, I will work to end it.*

Mrs. Hawthorne cleared her throat. "Perhaps, Mr. Sharp, you'd be so kind as to take Sarah up to make her congratulations to Minta now. I see that she and Hiram have stopped dancing for the time being, so this would be a good time."

"Of course." Calvin got immediately to his feet and offered Sarah his arm.

Beau got up, too. Obviously he meant to come along. "Oh, Beauregard," Mrs. Hawthorne said sweetly, putting out a hand to detain him. "Come sit over here by me. I want to speak to you about your dear mama. She's looking very—"

Calvin moved off, leaving behind what he was sure was a disgruntled Beau. "Have you told your mother about last night?" he leaned over to whisper to Sarah.

"No," Sarah whispered back, her eyes glowing warmly in the torchlight. "Not about us. But I think she suspects." She sighed. "Must you leave tomorrow? I so wanted some time to talk to you."

"As I did with you," he said. "But Beau is always there."

"I know. And I can't send him away without making Papa suspicious." She looked away from him, toward the dancers. Then she looked back and lowered her voice.

"If you could stay one more day, I might be able to get away to the slave quarters. Late in the afternoon when Beau's out riding with Papa. We might—we might be able to talk in Minta's cabin."

"I'd like that," he said, looking down into the beautiful face she turned to him. "I'd like it very much. But I don't want to get you in trouble."

"You won't." The smile she gave him made him feel ten feet tall. "I'll be careful. But now we'd better speak to Minta and get back to Mama. And to Beau." She frowned. "And you'd better think up a good excuse for staying another day."

He patted the hand that lay on his sleeve. "I will. Don't worry."

"Minta," Sarah cried, reaching out to grasp her hand and then Hiram's. "I'm so happy for you. I wish you and Hiram a lifetime of love."

"Thank you, Miss Sarah," Hiram said, his voice deep, his eyes shining. Up close, Calvin could see the intelligence in those dark eyes. Minta had made a good choice.

Minta searched Calvin's face and then gazed at Sarah. Minta smiled. "Maybe you have love too, Massa."

Calvin returned the smile. "Let's hope so."

He and Sarah turned back toward the others. "I'd like to walk off into the darkness with you," Calvin whispered. "And never come back. But I know we can't. I'll be in the slave quarters tomorrow afternoon after four. And don't worry; I've found a good excuse for staying another day."

By the time they got back to Mrs. Hawthorne and a clearly fuming Beau, they were discussing the warm Virginia weather. Beau vacated his seat with a frown and took up his position on the other side of Sarah again.

"So, Mr. Sharp," Mrs. Hawthorne asked. "What do you think of our holiday festivities?"

The warning was still in her eyes and he didn't ignore it. "Everyone seems to be having a lot of fun, including Willie." He heaved a sigh he hoped sounded genuine. "In fact, the way he's carrying on, I don't see how we'll be able to leave at dawn as I'd planned. I may have to impose on your hospitality for another day."

"That's quite all right," Mrs. Hawthorne said serenely, and he could have sworn she knew the truth, that she'd guessed that Sarah had taken his heart. "We always enjoy guests at Hawthorne Hill."

eleven

The next afternoon at four Sarah hurried toward the slave quarters. She'd hardly seen Calvin since lunchtime, and then she'd heard him tell Papa and Beau that since he was getting ready to leave in the morning, he wouldn't be riding with them this day. She'd kept herself from looking at him then by pretending he wasn't even there. Instead, she'd paid a lot of attention to Beau. And it had worked. Beau had smiled and preened himself, and then, when lunch was over, given her a peck on the cheek and ridden off with Papa, instead of staying there, trying to impress her.

She'd told Mama she was going to the quarters to see Minta and now, her heart pounding, she hurried along the path. If only Papa and Beau would stay out 'til later. She didn't want to do anything wrong with Calvin. She just wanted to talk to him. Well, maybe to have a hug from him. It was strange how a hug from Calvin could feel so different from one from Beau. But that must be the way it was with love.

Love. It was all so new to her, new and puzzling. She did love Calvin. It must be love if she wanted to spend the rest of her life with the man. But that was strange, too, because she'd never expected to love anyone. Oh, her children, yes. But she'd always thought they'd be Beau's children, too. And though she would love them, it wouldn't be a happy love, because she wouldn't love their father, and she knew they would grow up to be like him, to own slaves, to think

78

slavery was right and proper.

But that wasn't going to happen now. She would not marry Beau, not now that she knew what love was like. To be married to someone she didn't love would be so horrible she couldn't bear to think about it. Instead she'd think about Calvin, about having *his* children. That would be wonderful—a baby who looked like Calvin. Calvin would be a good husband and father. She knew it.

She hurried around a corner and almost ran into Willie coming toward her. Willie grinned. "Massa waiting, Miss Sarah. Most walked a rut in the floor already."

Willie paced beside her down the Row. Usually at this time of day the quarters were deserted; all the people were out in the fields working. But because it was holiday, there were a few about. She nodded to them and smiled. She had no fear they would say anything to Papa or Vickers, even if they knew she was meeting Calvin. Papa never listened to what slaves said anyway. He claimed everything they said was lies. Poor Papa. She was afraid for his immortal soul. And Vickers, no slaves went anywhere near him if they could help it. His soul must already be lost—he had been so wicked. But that was up to God to decide, not her.

Outside Minta's cabin she stopped, suddenly nervous, her stomach all butterflies. But that was silly. There was no reason to be nervous about Calvin. He was a good man. He would never hurt her.

"I wait here," Willie said. "Minta be out behind the cabin. Someone comes along the path, I sing." He demonstrated. " 'Foller, foller, rise up, shepherd, an' foller, foller the Star of Bethlehem.' I sing that, then Minta come in and warn you. Don't worry; you be safe."

She nodded. "Thank you, Willie."

Willie grinned. "Massa good to me. I do anything for him."

She stepped into the cabin and Calvin turned, his face alight. "Sarah."

She loved the way he said her name, as if it was something special. Then he took her hands and kept them in his own warm ones.

"I meant what I told you Christmas Eve," he whispered. "I want to marry you." A shadow crossed his face, his dear face. "But I don't know how or when."

"It's all right," she told him. "I'll wait for you. I'll wait however long it takes."

He frowned. "I wish I could at least send you some letters."

"I do, too," she said. "I want to know how you are." She hesitated, thinking. "I suppose you could write to Mama, at first to thank her for your visit, and later to let us know how Willie's doing. Papa would not take that amiss. Or suspect anything." She smiled at him. "And if Mama gets your letters then I will know you're all right."

"I will write to your mother, then," Calvin said, lifting her hands to lay them against the front of his coat. "But I wish I could tell you how much I love you."

She felt herself blushing, but she didn't care. "You don't have to do that," she said. "I see it in your eyes now. And I'll remember."

He smiled at her then. "You know, don't you, that I believe it was God who led me to the auction house that day, who led me to buy Willie?"

She hadn't known that he believed that, but she was glad he did. Surely she and Mama and Minta had prayed many, many prayers for Willie's safety. It wouldn't be strange if God had answered them.

Calvin chuckled. "No one was more surprised than me when I ended up with a slave. I'd never have imagined such a thing."

"It was a very good thing for Willie. He's changed so much."

"He'll change more," Calvin said. He looked around. Though the cabin was empty except for the two of them, he lowered his voice so she could barely hear him. "I'm teaching him to read. And when we get North, I'm going to see he gets schooling."

Her heart swelled with love. She'd been right about his goodness. "That will be marvelous," she said. "He's a very smart boy. He'll do well."

"I'm full of questions," he said, raising her hand to kiss her fingers. "I want to know all about you."

"There isn't much to tell," she said. "I've lived here all my life."

"How did you become involved in—" he looked toward the corner, toward the cornhusk mattress that covered the hidey-hole, "what you do?"

She smiled. "It's simple, Calvin. I'm against slavery. I always have been, as long as I can remember. If this place were mine, I'd free all the slaves. Right away."

He smiled. "I'm sure you would, my dear. But how did you come to such beliefs?"

"I learned them from Mama. She didn't always live in Virginia, you see. She was born and raised in Kentucky. And she used to hear a preacher there, a Reverend Rankin. He preached against slavery."

Calvin looked surprised. "Against? That must have made him very unpopular."

She nodded. "It did. So unpopular that finally he had to

move away. He went to Ohio, just across the river. And with his wife and sons—he has seven—he built a house that faces the river. A friend wrote to Mama that the lights in his windows can be seen from the riverbank. One of the Rankins is always watching the river, looking for runaways. If they see one, they help him or her on the way to freedom."

"On this mysterious Underground Railroad?" Calvin asked.

She nodded. "Yes. That's what Mama heard. We don't know much about it—only that it helps runaways go north."

"You don't know where the stations are?"

She shook her head. "Oh, no. We just know that one place to send runaways to. No place else."

"I suppose that's wise," Calvin said. "That way no one can give away the whole thing."

"Give away?" The thought was shocking. "Oh, no one would do that."

"Perhaps not," he said, patting her hand. "But it's sound policy, anyway."

She supposed he was right. "What about you?" she asked. "How did you—?"

"Hist!" Minta whispered from outside the window that had no glass. "I hear singing. Means Massa and Mr. Beau got back to the stables."

"I'll have to go," Sarah said. "But remember, Calvin, I love you and I'll wait for you." And she leaned toward him, hoping he would hug her. To her joy, he did. "I'll wait," she repeated, rising on tiptoes to put a kiss on his cheek. "I'll wait as long as it takes."

"I love you," he whispered. "Go now. I don't want you to get in trouble."

"I'll tell you good-bye now," she whispered, pulling out of his arms. "Because tomorrow I won't be able to do it properly. Godspeed."

His soft "Godspeed" followed her out the door and up the path toward the Big House. Calvin loved her. And she loved him. *Thank You, God,* she prayed. *Thank You for sending me Calvin.*

twelve

April 1860

The Virginia countryside was all abloom; wildflowers lined the roadside. Calvin pulled in lungsful of their fragrance. The smell of growing, new life was all around him. This was a beautiful place, much warmer than the Chicago they'd left still in the throes of winter's cold. The ride from Richmond had been pleasant, but it was Sarah he wanted to see. *His* Sarah.

At the end of the lane to Hawthorne Hill, he turned the rented horse toward the Big House. "We'll be there soon," he said to Willie, beside him on his own animal, leading the packhorse.

"Yes, Massa," Willie said, grinning. "Minta's going to be real glad to see me."

"Yes," Calvin said, "I'm sure she will."

Willie laughed. "Miss Sarah be glad to see you, too."

"I hope so," Calvin said, grinning back. She'd been sending little notes in with her mother's letters, but letters were different from being face-to-face.

It was hard to imagine what he would say to her. He longed to rush in and take her in his arms, to hold her close and never let her go. But that wasn't possible. They would have to go slowly and hide their feelings for each other until he could figure out some way to get her father's permission for them to marry. And that wasn't going to be easy.

He wasn't eager to face the colonel. The man saw too much. If he realized. . .

"You've grown a lot," Calvin said. Maybe making conversation with Willie would quiet his nerves.

"Yeah," Willie grinned, stretching out a foot. "Already had to get new boots."

Calvin nodded. "There's a lot new about you since we were here last."

Willie chuckled. "And the best of all is I can read." Though the road was empty, he looked around and lowered his voice. "You sure, Massa, you sure it's all right to tell Minta and Miss Sarah I can read?"

Calvin smiled. "Yes, it's all right. They won't tell anyone."

Willie nodded. "And they'll be real happy to know. Miss Sarah, she wanted to teach Minta, but Missus said someone might find out. And then they couldn't give the others help. You know," he looked around again, "maybe I can teach her."

"Maybe," Calvin said. "Just be careful."

Willie nodded, his face gone serious. "I will. Don't want the colonel to catch me."

They rode up to the Big House, its columns gleaming white in the sun. "Everybody been painting," Willie said. "Place looks all shiny."

They reined up at the veranda, and Joe hurried toward them. "Willie? That you agin?"

"It's me," Willie said. "Come back to visit. We on 'nother job for Mr. Pinkerton."

Joe's eyes grew big. He reached for the horses' bridles. "After you see Minta, you gonna come tell me 'bout it?"

"Sure," Willie said, slipping down from his horse. "I be there after a while."

Calvin swung down and smiled to himself. Though Willie was only eight, he had the makings of a first-rate operative. He could blend right in with his background. In the months they'd been gone, he'd learned how to speak properly—because he'd wanted to, not because anyone had pushed him to it. But now that they were here at Hawthorne Hill again, he'd dropped back into his slave patterns of speech and made his old friend more comfortable. Willie was a partner a man could depend on. Calvin knew. He already had.

As they approached it, the front door opened. "Good day, Mister Sharp," Albert said. His face was bland, but there was a certain look in his eyes that suggested that Albert knew more than he was saying. "Missus and Miss Sarah are in the west parlor." He glanced at Willie. "Minta will be there, too."

"Thank you, Albert," Willie said, making the old butler struggle to hold back a smile at this new grown-up Willie.

"And the colonel?" Calvin inquired, trying to sound nonchalant.

"The colonel rode over to the Gordons' this morning," Albert said. "We expect him back for dinner."

"Thank you." Calvin followed the butler into the Big House. Dinner. Maybe that meant he'd have a little time with Sarah. But he mustn't expect too much. He was a stranger here still, in spite of their letters. Too much a stranger.

Albert opened the door and stood aside. Calvin took a deep breath and stepped through.

"Good afternoon, Mr. Sharp." Mrs. Hawthorne smiled at him from her chair.

"Good afternoon, ma'am. It's good to see you again." Calvin managed to get the words out past the lump in his throat. He even managed to smile and nod at her. But then he finally let himself look at Sarah, let himself drink in the sight of her. How he'd longed for her smile over this long winter, longed for the sound of her sweet voice. "Good afternoon, Miss Hawthorne."

"Good afternoon, Mr. Sharp." Her face was calm, but there was the tiniest quiver in her voice. And her eyes were bright. Were those tears? Maybe of joy. He supposed she'd learned to hide her true feelings during these long years living in the midst of slaveholders, but he wished she could have dropped her needlework and run into his arms, to cover his face with kisses and tell him how much she missed him. Now he was being ridiculous. Sarah could never do that. She was a well-brought-up young lady.

"Sit down, Mr. Sharp," Mrs. Hawthorne said, nodding toward a chair. "Make yourself comfortable."

"Thank you, ma'am." Calvin took a chair, not next to Sarah, but where he could see her face. And only then did he see that Willie had run to Minta, and the two of them were sharing a big hug.

"How was your trip south?" Mrs. Hawthorne asked.

"The countryside is beautiful this time of year," Calvin said. "When we left Chicago, it was still cold and nasty there. Very cold and nasty."

Mrs. Hawthorne nodded. "I have never been North. At least, no further than Kentucky. I was raised there." She sighed. "I still get homesick sometimes—for the green fields and the horses."

Calvin nodded.

"And you, Mr. Sharp, where were you raised?"

"In Chicago, Mrs. Hawthorne. In the city. I'm afraid there were few horses and no green fields there." No need to mention the rest of it. He would tell Sarah about it later, when they were alone. *If* they were alone.

He swallowed. What would Mrs. Hawthorne say if he told her his mother had taken in washing? If he told her that from the age of seven he'd scoured the streets for odd jobs, any jobs that weren't illegal, to bring home the pennies that helped feed the younger children? Well, he would tell Sarah; he owed her that. But he didn't have to tell her mother, not yet, anyway.

Mrs. Hawthorne raised a hand to her mouth and yawned delicately. "My, look at the time. I'm feeling a little tired today. I believe I'll go lie upon my bed for a while before dinner."

Minta got up from where she was sitting on the floor, her arm around Willie, and started toward her.

"No, no, Minta," Mrs. Hawthorne said. "You stay here and visit with Willie. I'm quite able to manage alone."

"Thank you, Missus," Minta said, turning back to her brother.

Calvin sat there in his chair, hardly daring to breathe. Would Sarah go with her mother? Would her mother ask her to?

Mrs. Hawthorne smiled. "Sarah can see to it that you're given a proper room, Mr. Sharp. I hope you will be with us for a while. I'll see you at dinner." And she swept out the door, leaving him with his heart in his mouth.

Across the room, Sarah heard Mama's words, but it was seconds before she registered what they meant. Mama was leaving her alone with Calvin. Mama trusted him too. She got to her feet and took a step toward him. After all these months, he was really there, really right in front of her.

"I—" she began, her heart so full she could hardly speak,

"I am glad you could come to visit."

Calvin got up too and came toward her, but he didn't stop with one step. He came all the way, until he stood right in front of her. "I missed you," he said, his voice low. "I missed you so much."

"I missed you, too," she whispered, reaching out for his hands. They were just as strong and warm as she remembered them.

"Your mother," Calvin said. "Why did she leave us like that?"

"She trusts you," Sarah said. "As I do." She smiled at him. "I told Mama my feelings for you. I told her what you did to help—" Better not say it out loud, even if they were alone. "What you did on Christmas Eve."

Calvin nodded. "So that's why she sent your notes on to me. I wondered about that."

"Mama doesn't think Beau would make a good husband for me."

Calvin pulled her closer to him, until his eyes were only inches from her own. "Neither do I," he said. "I—oh, Sarah. Could I—? Do you mind if I kiss you?"

Her heart was pounding in her chest and her knees were weak as wilted greens, but she knew what she wanted.

"I don't mind," she whispered. "I think I would like—"

He didn't wait for any more words, but bent and kissed her. And it was wonderful, so much better than Beau's kisses that she could hardly believe it. When Beau kissed her, even on the cheek, she wanted to run off and wash her cheek, scrub it hard. But when Calvin kissed her, she wanted never to wash that place again.

She wanted to hold it forever in her heart—her first kiss from Calvin.

thirteen

A moment later Calvin led Sarah back to her chair and pulled one up beside her. She didn't know whether to be disappointed or relieved. But perhaps it was best this way. There were so many obstacles before them, so many problems to be overcome before they could marry.

"I must behave myself," Calvin said tenderly. "Your mother trusted me." He looked toward the door. "Albert said your father has gone to the Gordons."

"Yes," she said. "And I doubt that he'll be back for a couple more hours." She smiled at him and reached out to touch his sleeve. "We must make the most of it." She made a face. "Once Papa knows you're here, I suppose he'll have the Gordons over again. And then you and I will have no time to talk."

Calvin nodded. "There is so much I want to say to you."

She felt the heat rising to her cheeks and the words burst from her, "But first it's my turn."

"Of course," he said gravely. "What do you want to tell me?"

"I want to *ask* you," she said, "that day at the cabin I wanted to ask you, but I had to leave."

"Ask me anything you like," Calvin said. "I have no secrets from you." And his dark eyes gazed into hers with such tenderness that she felt wonderfully special.

"I told you about Mama, and about her hearing Reverend Rankin preach. But I want to know how you—" Her voice dropped to a whisper and without thinking she glanced at the door. "How you became an abolitionist?"

"I guess it really happened," he said, "that day at the auction house—when I saw poor scared-to-death Willie trying so hard to be brave." He reached out and took her fingers in his own. His strength seemed to flow through them to her. "Oh, I was already an abolitionist in principle, but when I saw that child, trying so hard to be brave, something snapped inside me." He smiled ruefully. "I certainly had no idea of buying a slave that day. I was after a counterfeiter and I'd traced him as far as Richmond. But I saw Willie look at Gordon. I saw the little fellow's knees trembling. And then my mouth opened, and out came my bid." He squeezed her fingers. "I was probably more surprised than anyone."

"You were the answer to our prayers," she said. She looked at him, just looked at him. He was here! He was really here.

He nodded. "I felt that God was behind what I did that day. I didn't understand why I was doing it, but I felt God was behind it."

She smiled. "Oh, Calvin, I'm so glad you're a believer. Now tell me about your family. I want to know about your growing up."

His eyes darkened with sadness. "I grew up when I was seven."

"Seven?" she asked in surprise.

"Yes. My father had a fondness for alcohol, you see." He paused, and a grimace of pain crossed his face. "Well, more like a passion. And one rainy night, befuddled by drink, he was run over by a wagon." He swallowed. "He died there in the muddy street."

Tears came to her eyes at such an awful story. "Oh, Calvin. I'm so sorry."

"At my father's grave, I promised my mother I would never touch alcohol. And I've kept my promise."

"But that isn't what you told—"

"I told the truth on Christmas Day," he said. "Mr. Pinkerton does have regulations against drinking." He shrugged. "I just saw no point in letting Beau know that I came up out of Chicago's slums."

"Slums?" she repeated. Surely he didn't mean those awful—

"Yes," he said. "From conditions not much better than those in Slave Row, I'm afraid. Though we were free. My mother took in washing to support the five of us. And I did whatever honest work I could find to bring home a penny or two to help."

"But you seem—" she faltered, unsure how to go on.

Calvin smiled and patted her hand. "It's all right, my dear. Say whatever you like."

"You seem like a gentleman." She glanced toward the corner where Willie and Minta huddled, whispering together. "And you can read and write."

"My mother felt very strongly about education. She made sure I could read and write. And cipher." He smiled. "I have to admit I was not as good a student as some I know." He, too, looked at Willie. "I was slow to see the value of learning. Too slow for my mother sometimes. But she insisted. She came from Scotland as a young woman, hoping for a new and better life in America. She lost that chance when my father became such a heavy drinker. But she was determined that all her children learn to read and write." He smiled wistfully. "And learn we did."

"Your mother sounds like a wonderful woman."

"She was." He sighed. "She passed away shortly after the youngest of us left home."

"I'm so sorry."

Calvin smiled sadly. "She told us not to grieve, that she was happy. She'd raised us all to adulthood—no mean task all by herself. She saw my sisters married to good men and my brothers employed in good jobs. She told us she'd done the work God had laid on her, and now she was ready to go." His voice grew husky. "I miss her a lot, especially these last days when I've been teaching Willie," he glanced around, and dropped his voice, "to read."

"Massa," Willie said, looking toward them and grinning. "Minta jest told me some good news."

Calvin smiled. "Then come here and tell me."

Willie ran over, still grinning. "Minta gonna have a baby! Come fall, I gonna be an uncle."

Calvin reached out and hugged the boy—and Willie hugged him back. Sarah swallowed over a lump in her throat. Except for the color of their skins, Willie could have been Calvin's son. No wonder Willie was so happy. Calvin was to him both father and friend.

"That's good news," Calvin said. "You'll be a fine uncle."

And you'll be a fine father, Sarah thought. *And maybe if Papa decides to sell Minta's baby, maybe I can get you to buy it.* But she mustn't think of that now. It would be months, even years, before they had to worry about that.

She leaned closer, putting a hand on his sleeve. "Tell me how Willie helped you catch the counterfeiter. That sounds fascinating."

"Wait!" Willie cried. "Minta's got to hear too." He grabbed

her hand and hurried her over.

"Well," Calvin said, as they sank to the floor at his feet. "It all began with these counterfeit banknotes. I'd been trailing this gang for weeks."

❧

Near dinnertime, the colonel returned and greeted Calvin with a jovial smile, then excused himself to do some work before the meal. Of course, by that time Mrs. Hawthorne had returned to the sitting room, and everything was perfectly proper. Calvin saw the glances that Sarah and her mother exchanged as the colonel left the room, but Calvin made polite conversation, discussing Chicago's weather and the ride south with Mrs. Hawthorne, and not the thing uppermost in his mind, and probably in theirs—had the colonel gone to send a message to Beau, to tell him the competition was at hand?

During dinner, Calvin let the colonel draw him out concerning the pursuit of certain criminals, counterfeiters in particular, but he avoided any mention of the Cooper case or Willie's part in it. If he had mentioned it, the colonel would only suspect him of sentimentality. Calvin smiled to himself. He hadn't exaggerated in telling the Cooper story to Sarah and Minta. Willie *had* saved his life.

Calvin refused a second portion of a pie made with pecans and brown sugar custard, and accepted a second cup of coffee. Then the door to the dining room opened, and Beau strode in as though he owned the place.

"Sit down, Beau," Mrs. Hawthorne said. "Have some pecan pie with us."

The invitation was only a formality, since before she even began to speak Beau had pulled out a chair and motioned to the waiting servant. Calvin looked to the colonel to see if he resented this usurpation of his authority, but the colonel was smiling happily. Evidently he didn't mind seeing Beau play lord of the manor, even though the manor wasn't Beau's.

Calvin glanced across the table to where Sarah toyed with her pie. Between bites of his, Beau launched into a diatribe against a lazy female slave who claimed she couldn't return to the fields even though she'd had a whole month to, as he put it, lay around since the birth of her baby. Sarah's face paled as Beau went on with a vivid description of the flogging the woman had received. Sarah's fork fell to the tablecloth, and she raised a trembling hand to her mouth.

"Really, Beau," Mrs. Hawthorne said, looking at him as though he were a little boy who'd spilled his milk. "That is hardly a fit subject for the dinner table. Can't you see you're upsetting Sarah?"

Beau laughed, a callous laugh that grated on Calvin's ears. What he wouldn't give to meet Beau with raised fists, teach him a little respect for womanhood. *Sorry, God. I know violence is not the answer.*

"Sarah has to know about these things sooner or later," Beau said with a shrug. "She's a planter's daughter and she's going to be a planter's wife."

He leaned closer to whisper in her ear, but Sarah turned her face away, her mouth grim. *Good for you,* Calvin thought. *If only I could make the man give you the respect you deserve.*

"Beau's right," the colonel said, eyeing Sarah. "I wasn't going to tell you 'til after we'd finished eating, but since you seem to be finished. . ."

Sarah looked up from her half-eaten pie and tried to smile. "Tell us what, Papa?"

"I am selling Hiram south."

Sarah gave a little gasp and fell back in her chair, her face gone even paler. A moment later she straightened. "But why, Papa?"

"It's his own fault," the colonel said. "Vickers came to me about a slave who wouldn't work, a lazy fellow called Brutus."

Calvin swallowed. No doubt the same Brutus who'd been in trouble last fall.

"Vickers ordered Hiram to give this Brutus the lash," the colonel went on. "He saw Brutus chained up to the whipping post, then headed back to his cabin for another bottle." He glanced at Calvin. "Perhaps Mr. Pinkerton has the right idea. The bottle has certainly not improved Vickers's performance on the job. At any rate, Vickers went back to his cabin to the happy accompaniment of howls of pain from the slave who was being whipped. But halfway there he realized he'd dropped something; I believe he said a coin of some kind, and he went back to get it."

"And what happened then?" Beau asked, helping himself to a third piece of pie.

The colonel shrugged. "Vickers discovered that though Brutus was chained up and howling like the skin was being stripped from him, Hiram wasn't flogging the fellow at all. He was flogging another post. An empty post."

The colonel looked at Calvin, but Calvin kept his face impassive. *Good for Hiram. And Beau thought slaves were stupid.* But Calvin wouldn't jeopardize his welcome by coming to Hiram's defense. It was useless anyway. The colonel would not take advice from a Northerner.

"Instead of interfering," the colonel went on, "and letting Hiram know he'd been found out, Vickers came to me. I told him to keep silent on the matter until I had made up my mind."

From the corner of his eye, Calvin saw Willie sidle away and slip out the half-open door.

"Vickers suggested selling them both south," the colonel went on. "And I believe that's what I'll do. Brutus has been nothing but trouble. And this behavior of Hiram's is outrageous."

"That's the idea," Beau said. "Get rid of 'em both. Too bad you can't have 'em flogged first, but they wouldn't bring as much that way."

Sarah glanced at her mother, but Mrs. Hawthorne's face was serene. She couldn't feel as she looked, but she'd had many years to learn to hide her emotions. Sarah looked at her father. "Papa?"

"Yes?"

"I've heard you say that Hiram has been a very good driver. That his crew brings in a lot of cotton."

The colonel nodded. "That's true, my dear."

"Won't it be difficult for his crew to do as well for someone else? Won't you be losing a lot of money if you sell him?"

The colonel looked thoughtful. Calvin held his breath. Sarah knew how to aim an appeal to her father, not at humanity or decency, but at profit. Would she succeed?

"That's true," the colonel said finally. "Perhaps—"

But Beau shook his head and slapped the table with the flat of his hand. "You can't allow this kind of thing. If you do, they'll turn lazy on you. The whole lot of 'em."

Sarah faced him for a moment, anger in her eyes. Then she turned back to her father. "But, Papa, surely one mistake—"

"One mistake is all it takes," Beau said, threat in his

voice, and it was clear he wasn't just talking about Hiram.

Sarah's expression turned pleading. "Please, Papa. I am asking you—give Hiram another chance. I'll speak to Minta. Surely she can—"

"It won't work," Beau said. "You got to teach them a lesson."

Silence settled over the room. Calvin tried to look as though none of this mattered to him.

"Beau's right," the colonel said finally. "I can't allow this kind of thing. The slaver will be by tomorrow. Vickers said he'd send for him. They're both going south."

Calvin's heart fell at the look of utter despair settling on Sarah's face. She pushed her chair back from the table. "I'm not feeling good," she mumbled. "Please excuse me." She was so pale, he felt his heart contract. His hands went to his chair, but he stopped himself. He had no right to go to her.

"Here, let me help you," Beau began, putting down his fork.

"No! That is, I'm just going up to my room. I'll be fine." And she rose and hurried off.

Calvin watched her go, fighting the urge to follow, to comfort her. He had no right. And her father wouldn't like it—to say nothing of Beau.

But Sarah would not give in this easily. He had a strong suspicion it was not to her bed that she was going, but to alert Minta.

Willie had been standing behind her, so she hadn't seen him slip out. But unless Calvin missed his guess, Minta knew the truth by now. There would be a lot of grieving in the little cabin that night when Minta and Hiram made their good-byes.

Calvin sipped his coffee. He seriously doubted that the slaver would find Hiram or Brutus when he arrived at Hawthorne Hill on the morrow.

fourteen

Sarah hurried from the dining room, her heart pounding in her throat. It was wrong to hate. She knew that. Jesus had said to love your enemies. But she couldn't. Not now. She hated Beauregard Gordon! How could the man be so cruel? He actually seemed to take pleasure in tormenting her, first with that story about the poor woman he'd had flogged because she couldn't work. And then—just when she'd about had Papa talked into giving Hiram another chance—Beau had ruined that. Now Hiram and Minta would be separated, and it was all Beau's fault. She would never marry such a man. She'd die first!

She gathered her skirts and hurried up the broad staircase. She had to find Minta, find her right away so she could warn Hiram. Papa evidently meant to allow them one last night together, but she didn't think they should wait. Hiram should start north immediately, before Beau persuaded Papa that Hiram should be locked up for the night. That was just the sort of thing Beau would do. Yes, Hiram had to leave—and soon.

If only Mr. Ferris hadn't fallen ill this winter and died. Now they didn't know where to send runaways. And no one had gotten them word yet about a new Underground station. They could only give the runaways some food and point them in the right direction.

She reached the top of the stairs and hurried toward her room. Maybe Minta was in there, putting things to rights.

She pushed open the door. "Minta, I just—"

Minta was putting clean clothes in a drawer, her back to the door. She turned, tears rolling down her cheeks. "Massa selling my Hiram south."

Sarah sat down suddenly. Her knees felt like they wouldn't hold her. "How did you know?"

"Willie hear the colonel tell you. He come tell me."

"And you told Hiram?"

Minta sniffled. "Willie went. Said he could do it without getting caught." Minta wiped her eyes. "Hiram got to go North now, but Massa Ferris ain't there no more to help."

"I know," Sarah said. "What are we going to do?"

"I don't know. I jest knows I feel awful." And Minta burst into tears.

Sarah got up and went to put her arms around her.

Finally Minta said, "You 'spose Massa Calvin'd buy my Hiram?"

Tears rose to Sarah's eyes. "He would if he could, Minta. I know he would. But Hiram must be worth fourteen or fifteen hundred dollars. Pinkerton men don't make that kind of money. And Calvin's family wasn't well-to-do."

Minta nodded. "I 'spected that. Massa Calvin don't act like no rich man. Hiram got to go North, then. That's all that's left to do."

"Maybe. . .maybe you should go with him," Sarah said, making herself say the words though her heart felt as if it would break in two. She didn't know what she'd do without Minta. Minta had always been there, from the time they were little girls. But she had to think about Minta, too, not just herself. "Hiram loves you so much. There's the baby to think of and—"

"I knows." Minta sighed. "But iffen I go North, there

won't be no one here to help you. Missus can't do it no more. She too sick. And runaways can't come right to the Big House."

Minta was right. If she left, the Underground would lose another stopping place.

Tears started to roll down Minta's face again. Sarah hugged her close. "Don't cry, Minta. He can't buy Hiram, but I know Calvin will help us. Surely he can think of something. Some way to get Hiram away safe."

"I hopes so," Minta said, turning to her with a pleading face. "Miss Sarah." She took Sarah by the hand. "Miss Sarah, let's pray to the Lord Jesus 'bout this."

"Of course," Sarah said. "Let's pray now." And they went down on their knees.

≈

When his coffee cup was empty, Calvin looked around the table. "If you'll excuse me, I have to finish my report to Mr. Pinkerton."

"Of course," Mrs. Hawthorne said. "You will join us in the parlor for some music later, won't you? After you finish?"

Her voice was pleasant enough, but he read warning in her eyes. If he interpreted it correctly, her look meant "stay away from Sarah tonight." "Yes, Mrs. Hawthorne. I'd like that."

He nodded to the colonel and Beau, and made his exit. He had to find Willie. But first he had to go to his room and produce the report, so he could give it to the colonel to be mailed. The colonel was a stickler for detail. It wouldn't do to make him suspicious.

Fortunately, Calvin thought, making his way up the stairs and toward his room, *the report only needs a few more lines.* There would be time to confer with Willie, if he could find him.

He pushed open the door to his room. First, the report and then—Willie was curled up on the floor, sobbing. Calvin knelt beside him and put a hand on his shoulder. "Willie, come on now. Don't cry. Hiram will be all right."

Willie looked up, tears streaming down his face. "You heard—Colonel gonna—sell Hiram—south—Minta never—see him—no more—He never—get to—see the—baby."

"But he can go North," Calvin said. "You can lead him to the next station."

Willie shook his head. "Can't now." He sat up and sniffled. "Minta say Mr. Ferris, he die. And ain't no one come to tell her next place to send folks."

His heart sinking, Calvin settled in his chair. He hadn't thought about something like that happening. He lifted Mother's Bible from the table nearby. Just holding it in his hands comforted him, making him feel closer to God. "Willie, stop crying now. We have to think."

Willie sniffed a few more times, but he stopped crying. "What we thinking 'bout, Massa?"

"How to save Hiram, of course."

Willie's face lit up. "You could buy him like you did me."

Calvin shook his head. "I'm sorry, Willie, but I can't. I don't have the money."

Willie's face fell. "What we gonna do? I *been* thinking. And thinking some more. But I can't think of nothing."

Calvin smoothed the worn cover of the Bible. "Maybe we should pray," he said.

Willie got to his knees. "Yes, Massa. We ask God to help us."

Calvin knelt and bowed his head. "Dear Father in heaven, we need Your help to save Hiram. Hiram is a good man, one of Your children. But You know that. Please help us to think of a way to save him. Thank You. And Your will be done."

Calvin raised his head. An idea was forming in his mind. "Willie?"

Willie looked up, his eyes gleaming with more tears. "Yes, Massa?"

"Listen carefully now. I want you to go find Miss Sarah. When no one else can hear, tell her I said her mother's got to get sick tonight, so sick Minta has to stay with her all night. Here in the Big House. And tell them to be sure they make a lot of noise, so the colonel knows she's there all night."

Willie nodded. "I tell her."

"And tell Minta that Hiram should leave right after dark. Just in case."

Willie nodded again. "I tell him. But where he gonna go?"

"Tell him to go south."

Willie's eyes got wide. "South, Massa?"

"Yes, the patrollers won't look south. He can go to Edgerton's. You know, where we stopped the day before we came here. You can tell Hiram how to get there. Edgerton's an old Pinkerton man, a friend of mine, you know. Tell Hiram to take Brutus and go there. Tell him to mention my name. Edgerton will hide them. In a week or so, when we leave here, we'll swing by there and pick them up. By then we'll have something figured out. A way to get them north to freedom."

"Yes, Massa," Willie said, wiping at the tears on his cheeks. "I tell 'em. I tell 'em everything you say. I tell Minta it's gonna be all right." He pulled on his boots and stood up. "Tonight, will you read me that story in the Bible agin? That one 'bout Moses?"

Calvin swallowed over the lump in his throat. "You mean the one that says, 'Let my people go'?"

"That's the one, Massa. That's the one." And Willie was out the door. With a sigh, Calvin turned to his report.

An hour later, Calvin went down to the parlor where the others were gathered. First he crossed to the colonel. "I'd appreciate it if you'd send this off for me," he said, handing him the envelope. "Mr. Pinkerton likes reports to come in on time."

The colonel nodded. "Of course. I'll have it taken to Richmond in the morning."

"Thank you."

Then Calvin allowed himself to glance around the room. Sarah sat in a corner, her face pale but composed. She didn't look at him. But that was to be expected. The less interest they showed in each other the better.

Beau sat beside her, of course. He was whispering something and grinning, but Sarah didn't respond to him. Her face remained set in lines of sorrow. "Come on," Beau said loudly. "All this fuss about a slave is stupid. Snap out of it now."

Sarah still didn't answer him, but turned to her mother. "Mama, would you play us a song?"

"I'm terribly tired tonight, my dear," Mrs. Hawthorne said. "Perhaps you'd better play."

Sarah looked worried. "All right, Mama. If you wish."

Mrs. Hawthorne looked pale. Calvin wasn't sure if it was put on or if she was really ill. But she leaned back in her chair and sighed.

"Are you feeling worse?" Sarah asked, coming to her side.

Mrs. Hawthorne smiled. "No, dear. I'm all right. Go play a song for us."

"Yes, Mama."

"Play that one Mr. Foster wrote, the one about Kentucky. And sing it for us, please."

"Yes, Mama." Sarah settled at the piano and smoothed her skirts around her. Calvin supposed it was all right to look at her while she was playing. He'd be careful to seem bored. That wouldn't be an easy job, though, especially tonight when every nerve in his body was jumping and his mind was a jumble of thoughts. Had Hiram and Brutus gotten away? Would they make it to Edgerton's? Did the colonel suspect anything?

Trust in God, Calvin told himself. *It's as Mother said. You've done all you could. Now you've got to trust in God.*

The song Sarah began was sad and wistful, her voice low and melodious. "Oh, the sun shines bright on my old Kentucky home, My old Kentucky home so far away."

Several times Calvin was aware of the colonel looking at him speculatively, but probably it was just because he was a Northerner. The colonel couldn't know anything. Willie hadn't been caught seeing Hiram. At that very moment Willie was standing behind Calvin's chair, waiting in case his master should need anything. But the colonel could be playing the waiting game with them, too. As he had with Hiram.

Calvin swallowed a sigh. This kind of thinking would get them nowhere. He tried to concentrate on Sarah's playing.

She finished the piece and started to look for another.

"Sarah," Mrs. Hawthorne said. "I believe I'd better go up now."

Sarah left the piano immediately. "Of course, Mama."

The colonel stood and looked at his wife with what seemed like genuine affection. "You tire yourself, my dear. You rest now."

Mrs. Hawthorne smiled wanly. "Yes, I will."

Calvin watched them go out. He longed to go and help Sarah, to be there for her. But that was impossible.

The colonel sank down in his chair. "She's delicate, my wife."

"I'll pray for her recovery," Calvin said.

The colonel gave him an odd look. "She takes these spells, that's all." He took out his cheroot case and offered it to Beau. Beau took one and sniffed appreciatively. The colonel turned to Calvin, then closed the case. "Sorry; I forgot you don't indulge."

Calvin managed a smile. "It's been a long day. I did a lot of riding, too. I believe I'll leave you gentlemen to your smokes and bourbon, and retire early. Good night. And thank you, Colonel, for your hospitality."

The colonel nodded and lit up his cheroot. "Good night, Mr. Sharp."

fifteen

When they started downstairs in the morning, Calvin warned Willie. "You don't know anything about Hiram running away," he reminded him. "Nothing at all."

Willie nodded. "I know, Massa."

Long before they reached the breakfast room, they could hear the sound of shouting. At the door, Calvin sent Willie a warning glance and stepped into the room.

"I told you, Colonel," Beau said, slamming a fist on the table for emphasis. "You're too easy on 'em. Far too easy. When they catch 'em, you ought to whip 'em within an inch of their lives."

"Has something happened?" Calvin asked, blessing the training that had taught him not to let his face show his emotions, and praying Willie could play his part as well. Willie had done a good job in the Cooper affair, but this was more personal, closer to his heart.

"Yes, Mr. Sharp," the colonel said, looking up, "something *is* wrong. Hiram and Brutus have run away."

"Run away?" Calvin repeated, hoping that he sounded surprised.

"Yes," Beau cried, his face twisting with anger. "The savages have run off. But they'll soon learn. There's no one out there to give them food and shelter. They're too stupid to get along on their own. They'll get caught. Or they'll be back."

Calvin took a plate from the sideboard and helped himself to the food. Did Beau really believe that Hiram would

108

come back? To be sold south away from his wife and child? Calvin kept his face turned from the colonel and Beau. He supposed he ought to say something, but he just didn't know what to say. Maybe it was better just to keep silent and eat.

He was ladling eggs on his plate when Beau said gruffly, "Boy, come over here."

His heart in his throat, Calvin turned. There had been no boys in the room when he came in, no boys but Willie. Willie was crossing the room toward Beau. Willie stood in front of him, head bent, gaze on the floor as a slave's should be.

Calvin swallowed. What did Beau want with Willie? He didn't like the sound of this. Maybe he should send the boy out of the room now. But that could look suspicious, and they didn't need that. They had to be extra careful. That's why he hadn't sent Willie away from him before.

"Now, boy," Beau said, his tone stern, his face thunderous. "Look at me."

Willie looked into Beau's face. "Yes, Massa?" His voice was rock steady.

"Minta's your sister, isn't she?"

Willie slowly nodded. "Yes, Massa."

"And she's Hiram's wife."

"Yes, Massa." Willie's voice had started to tremble.

Please, God, Calvin prayed, *show me what to do. Show me how to help him.*

"Then she must know where Hiram went."

Willie hesitated, then he said, "No, Massa. She don't know. She been with Missus. Missus been sick."

"He's right," the colonel said. "She was here all night. I heard her and Sarah."

Beau shot out an arm and grabbed Willie by the shirt-front, hauling him closer. "You know!" he thundered, shaking the boy roughly. "And you'll tell me now. Or I'll beat it out of you! I swear I'll do it myself!"

Willie didn't make a peep. He just hung there, his feet an inch off the floor, suspended by Beau's grip.

Calvin set his plate down on the sideboard with a thump and stepped to the table. "Excuse me," he said, his voice harsh. He looked pointedly at the fist that still clutched Willie's shirtfront. "I believe that is my property you're manhandling. Mine."

Beau released Willie's shirt, and Willie's feet hit the floor. He struggled and managed to stay erect, staring downward, his shoulders bent. Beau glared up at Calvin. "But I'm telling you this boy knows where—"

"This—boy—knows—nothing," Calvin said, emphasizing each word and begging silent forgiveness for the lie. "This boy sleeps in my room. He was there all night. He knows nothing."

Beau came to his feet and glared straight into Calvin's face. "I'm telling you, Sharp, this boy knows where Hiram went. Just let me have him for an hour and—"

And he'll be dead, Calvin thought. He stiffened and glared back at Beau. "Mr. Gordon, it sounds suspiciously like you're calling me a liar." He lowered his voice, investing it with all the threat he could. These Southerners were much concerned with their "honor." They believed in the code duello. "And if you are calling me a liar, I mean to insist on satisfaction."

He wasn't about to fight for his so-called honor, not the kind Beau espoused at any rate. But Willie's life was something else, something more precious than any man's honor.

"Well, ah—" Beau began, surprise on his face. His voice faded away.

Calvin waited. If he had to fight Beau, he would. Though as a Christian he tried to avoid fighting, he was as good a shot as any. And no man was going to beat Willie while Calvin Sharp was alive.

"I still think," Beau said, though in a more placating voice, "that—"

"Oh, sit down, Beau," the colonel said. And when Beau didn't move, the colonel repeated his words, more sharply. "Sit down and let the man be. The fact that Hiram is gone doesn't mean the boy had any part of it." He poured himself some more coffee. "Besides, they'll catch Hiram. I put out a five-hundred-dollar reward for him. He'll never make it North."

Watching Willie's back, Calvin saw his shoulders quiver. The boy couldn't take much more. "Willie," he said. "I left my plate on the sideboard. Finish filling it and bring it here."

"Yes, Massa," Willie said. His voice was steadier now. What bravery the boy had shown. Beau would have beaten him; that much was clear. A grown man beating a child. And thinking it was right! *Oh, Lord, this is so wrong. So terribly wrong.*

Calvin pulled out a chair and sat down. "I'm sorry you're having problems, Colonel," he said. Well, that wasn't really a lie. "But I'm sure you can understand my feelings in the matter. I don't appreciate having my word doubted. And as for beating my slave— What's mine is mine. No one damages my property."

It bothered him to speak of Willie that way, as a thing to be owned, but it was all these people could understand.

Willie had to be protected.

The colonel shrugged. "I would expect nothing else. I'm afraid Beau here is rather used to having his own way. He doesn't often get thwarted."

Calvin nodded and poured himself a cup of coffee. His hand was steady as he raised the cup to his lips. A Pinkerton operative had nerves of steel.

When Willie put a full plate in front of him, Calvin glanced up. Willie's face was expressionless, but his eyes were bright and his lower lip quivered, just once.

"Go out to the kitchen now," Calvin said, "and get your own breakfast. I don't need you in here."

"Yes, Massa," Willie said, and his eyes added a thank you. Slowly and steadily he crossed the room and went out the door. *A real trooper, Willie.*

Calvin was pouring a second cup of coffee when the door opened again. He looked up, and there was Sarah, moving slowly into the room. She looked paler than usual, her violet eyes huge in her face.

The colonel looked up, too. "How is your mother this morning?" he asked.

"She's sleeping now, Papa. I think she's some better. But she had an awful night." She turned to the sideboard. "Before she dozed off, she told me to come down and get some breakfast."

The colonel nodded and went back to his coffee. Sarah picked up a plate. Only then did she glance at Calvin, and then only for a moment, but he saw the question in her eyes. He didn't dare to answer it. He didn't even dare to smile, not with Beau sitting there.

"Have you heard the news?" Beau asked her, malice in his voice.

She brushed wearily at her eyes. "Not now, Beau, please. I hardly slept a wink last night. Mama was very ill." And she turned to the sideboard, effectively putting her back to him.

But nothing could stop Beau. Evidently, he thought his news would hurt her. "I was right to tell your father to sell Hiram south. The fool ran away last night. Now your father's lost a lot of money."

For the space of three seconds Sarah stood stock-still, then she began putting food on her plate again. When she turned, her face was composed. "I'm sorry, Papa. I know Hiram was worth a lot of money."

The colonel nodded. "He'll be caught. He's not smart enough to make it North. They'll both be caught."

"Yes, Papa. I'm sure they will." Sarah took a seat at the table, a seat near her father, not near Calvin.

Sarah stared down at her plate, a plateful of food she didn't really want. But she had to pretend to be hungry, just as she had to pretend about last night. It was hard work to pretend. It had been a difficult night, pretending to help Minta with Mama. Truth to tell, they hadn't had to pretend much. All three of them had been half sick with worry and fear, wondering if Hiram would make it away, or if Beau had thought to get Papa to lock Hiram up early.

They'd spent all night wondering and worrying—Minta fussing about Willie's part in the whole thing and whether he'd get in trouble for it, and worrying about Hiram, and grieving because they were going to be separated, and she hadn't even gotten to tell him a proper good-bye.

Sarah took a forkful of eggs, forcing them past the lump in her throat. She had worried about Hiram, Willie, and Minta, but most of all she had worried about Calvin. If

Papa ever discovered Calvin's true sympathies lay with the abolitionists, there would be no chance for them to marry. That wouldn't stop Calvin, of course. He would do what was right in the sight of God. He would always do what was right in the sight of God, even if it cost him everything, including her.

She allowed herself one little glance at him, one tiny glance, and then she looked away again. She didn't dare look at him for long. Papa might notice. Or Beau. They might see the love she felt. She picked up her cup and raised it to her lips. No one must see that she loved Calvin. No one.

sixteen

September 1860

"Oh, Miss Sarah," Minta moaned, twisting and turning on the cornhusk mattress, her fingers clutching at the quilt that she'd made for her marriage bed. "How much longer you think it gonna be? Don't seem like it oughta take so long."

Sarah turned from the hearth where she was adding a log to the fire, and pushed a strand of hair back from her forehead. "I don't know, Minta. I wish I did."

Minta was right. It had been a long labor—and difficult. Mama had been too ill to come and help. So Sarah had had to manage by herself. Well, Lucy had been there for a while, but Sarah had sent her off to rest. She could help later. And besides, when Lucy was there, it was harder to talk. And talking seemed to help Minta. Between the pains, at least.

Sarah closed her eyes. *Please, God, help Minta's baby to be born. I've done all I know how to do.*

She went back to the mattress and dipped a cloth in the bucket of cool water to wipe Minta's face. Having a baby was always hard work, but this one seemed to be taking longer than it should.

"I wisht Hiram was here," Minta whispered. "I miss him somethin' terrible."

"I know," Sarah said. "I miss Calvin." She wasn't married to Calvin, but she still missed him. Funny how she could miss a man she'd only spent about two weeks with altogether. But she did miss him. It was as if a part of her was gone, cut away. And she would not be really whole again until she was with him.

But there was no use in thinking such thoughts. Things would happen in God's own time. She just had to do her duty and trust in God. At least Calvin had gotten Hiram and Brutus away to freedom. She and Minta had prayed and prayed, and waited and waited. And finally the letter had come.

"At least Hiram safe," Minta said. "He won't be slave no more."

"That's right," Sarah said, straightening wearily. She had an awful crick in her back, and her head was pounding, but she wasn't going to leave Minta, not until the baby was safely born.

"Tell me agin," Minta said, breathing heavily. "Tell me how Massa Calvin got 'em away. I likes to hear that story."

Sarah smiled. "I like it, too."

"Tell me agin," Minta said. "While I resting."

"Yes," Sarah said, wringing out the cloth. "I will. You remember, Calvin sent a letter to Mama, a letter thanking us for our hospitality. And then he put in that separate sheet, one that repeated the story he said he'd seen in the paper."

Minta groaned. "Wait. I gotta push."

Sarah waited, holding Minta's hands while she pushed. When the pain had passed, Sarah went on. "I remember it word for word." She recited it. " 'Two male slaves escaped recently by riding the train from Richmond to Philadelphia, and then to Chicago. They were wearing women's apparel, including women's bonnets, and carrying false papers. They were big women, but no one said anything to them, except for one conductor, who got suspicious. But while he was questioning them, there was some commotion in the other end of the car, caused, it seems, by a slave boy, who was caught stealing coins out of his master's pocket. By the time this was settled, they had reached Philadelphia and the conductor was too busy to ask any more questions.' "

Minta smiled in spite of her pain. "That Willie a marvelous good boy."

"Yes," Sarah said. "He is. We were doubly blessed the day God sent Calvin to buy him."

"Yeah. Ahhhhhh!"

"Push, Minta! Push." Sarah knelt beside the mattress. "I see it! I see the baby's head! It'll be real soon now."

"Praise the Lord," Minta groaned, when that pain had passed. "I be hurting bad, Miss Sarah. I was afeared I wouldn't make it through this."

"You will," Sarah said, over the lump in her throat. "You have to."

"But my baby—" Tears ran down Minta's cheeks. "My baby gonna be slave. Anytime he want, the colonel kin sell my baby. Or me."

"I know, Minta. I know. But we can't worry about that now. We've got to get the baby born."

Minta nodded, her eyes bright. "You right, Miss Sarah. This baby got to be borned. Here comes another 'un. Ahhhhhhhhh!"

"Just a few more pushes," Sarah said. "Hiram will be so proud of you. Mama will send word to Calvin, and he'll tell Willie. Maybe Willie will be able to read the news for himself. And they'll get word to Hiram. Push now! It's coming!"

Half an hour later, Sarah wrapped the squalling baby in a clean flour sack and looked down into her tiny dark face. "I promise you, Minta's baby, I won't let you be sold away from your mama. Not if I have to run off with you myself," she finished, hugging her fiercely.

She knelt to put the precious bundle in Minta's waiting arms. "What will you call her?" she asked. "I got Papa to say you could give her a name."

Minta looked up. "Bessie. That's what I'll call her. You go to bed now, Miss Sarah. You brought my baby into the world." Her eyelids fluttered closed, then opened again. "Me and Bessie be all right now. Praise the Lord Jesus. You kin call Lucy to come sit with me. You got to sleep. You got to take care of your mama 'til I gets better." A smile crossed Minta's weary face. "And you got to write a letter. Praise God; now you can write that letter."

Sarah trudged up the path to the Big House, her steps heavy, but her heart light. Thank God, it had been a safe delivery. She'd been real worried for a while there. The baby's birth seemed to be taking so long, too long. She'd never delivered a baby all by herself before, but she'd helped Mama many times.

She'd wanted Minta to have her baby in the house, but Minta had said she'd rather be in her own cabin, on the cornhusk mattress she'd shared with Hiram. She felt closest to him there. And Sarah could understand that. She sighed and rubbed at her back. It felt as if she were permanently bent over, and she was bone-weary. But then, she'd been up all night. Now she wanted to get upstairs and go to bed. If she could just get in without Papa seeing her, that's what she would do.

She would take off her dirty clothes and wash her face and

hands, and crawl gratefully into bed. Then she would close her eyes and think about Calvin. She would pray for him, as she had prayed for him every night since she'd met him, pray that God would keep him safe and bring him back to her.

She pushed open the back door and stepped inside. If only no one saw her come— But Albert was there, waiting. "The colonel is looking for you, Miss Sarah," Albert said, his eyes worried. "He said to send you to the dining room the very minute you come in."

Sarah looked down at her soiled gown and dirty hands. "I'd better wash first," she said.

Albert shook his head. "Don't think you better, Miss Sarah. Mr. Beau with the colonel. Mr. Beau upset."

Sarah sighed. Beau was always upset. And always pushing at her to get married. But she wasn't going to do it. Not now. Now that she knew what love was really like, marrying Beau would be so wrong.

"Thank you, Albert; I'll go right in." She was a mess, her gown dirty, her hair straggling. She paused. Maybe seeing her like this would put Beau off. She swiped a hand across her face, hoping to leave it even dirtier. But it probably wouldn't do any good. After all, it wasn't her that Beau wanted as much as it was the land and the slaves that went with it. It was Hawthorne Hill he was after, and he had to marry her to get it. Enough thinking. She might as well go and get this over with.

She went down the hall and pushed open the dining room door. "Good morning, Papa."

Beau had better stop eating so much or he was going to look like his father. "I would have cleaned up," she said, addressing herself to Papa. "But Albert said you wanted to see me right away. Is something wrong with Mama?"

"No," Papa said. "Your mother is all right."

Sarah heaved a sigh of relief. "Thank goodness. I told Lucy's girl to come for me if Mama needed me."

"What were you doing?" Papa asked, his gaze probing her face.

"Minta was having her baby," she said, glad she didn't have to lie under his scrutiny. She hardly ever lied. It was wrong and she didn't like to do it. And, besides that, she wasn't good at it. "And I wanted to be there."

"That ain't fitting work for a lady," Beau declared between bites. "Birthing slave babies, that's dirty business. Ought to leave it to slaves."

She kept her distaste off her face, but it was hard. Beau was such a pig. *How could God possibly love—?* But she couldn't be thinking about that now. "I thought you would want the baby safely delivered," she said to Papa. "And she was. Bessie's a strong healthy baby. She'll serve us well."

She almost choked on that last part, but she got it out. She couldn't let Papa suspect her real feelings, but she couldn't quite say, "She'll be worth a lot."

Papa nodded, seeming satisfied. "That's good. But in the future maybe you'd better let one of the slaves do that kind of thing."

"Yes, Papa." She wasn't lying then, either. Minta wouldn't be having any more babies with Hiram gone. And Lucy knew how to deliver babies as well as Sarah did. Better.

"Get yourself some breakfast," Papa said. "And then go rest a while."

"Maybe I should wash first," she said. "At least my hands."

"Miss Sarah," Albert said from behind her. "Here's a wet cloth to wash up with."

"Thank you, Albert. That was very thoughtful of you."

She saw Beau's eyes widen. He didn't think it was proper to thank a servant. He thought they should just be there and anticipate his every wish. But she was through caring what he thought. She cleaned her hands, gave the cloth back to Albert, and turned to the sideboard.

She really didn't want to deal with Beau this morning. Of course, she didn't want to deal with Beau any morning. He was rude and overbearing, sometimes really obnoxious, and the thought of being his wife, which had been uncomfortable before, was now unbearable. It was hard to believe that she'd ever actually considered marrying him.

She took her filled plate to the table and sat down near Papa. Papa smiled at her, but it was the smile she'd learned to dislike, the one she knew meant he wanted her to do something she didn't really want to do.

"Beau is here for a purpose," Papa said.

Her heart fell. The same old purpose, she supposed. Beau was really eager for their marriage to take place. But she put a smile on her face. "Oh, have you bought a new horse, Beau? And brought him over for us to see? Is it a stallion or—?"

"No."

She took a mouthful of bacon, forced herself to chew it slowly, to swallow. Then she asked, "I hope your mother's not ill?"

"No." Now Beau was scowling. Well, let him scowl. She wasn't going to bring up the subject of their wedding. Not if he sat there scowling forever. "You know very well why I'm here," he said, slamming down his fork.

She shook her head. "No, I'm afraid I don't. You'll have to excuse me, Beau. I'm half asleep this morning."

This time it was his fist that Beau slammed down, hitting the table with such force that the dishes jumped. "Sarah Hawthorne! You know very well I'm here to get you to set a date for our wedding. I've been waiting long enough. It's time we got it done."

"Oh." She pretended to be surprised. Done! As if it were a piece of work or something. "I didn't know you were talking about our wedding."

"What else?" Beau scowled even harder.

"Well, I haven't settled on a date yet." She didn't like to half lie like this, but she had to keep putting him off until Calvin could think of something. "Mama hasn't been well, you know. And I don't like to think of leaving her."

Beau shrugged. "Your father has plenty of slaves. Let them look after her."

For some reason, she turned to look at Papa. And her breath caught in her throat. Papa's face had darkened. He didn't like Beau to talk about Mama like that. In his own way, Papa loved Mama. She'd always known that. Maybe. . .

"But I'm her daughter," she went on. "No one cares about her as I do. I couldn't leave her alone when she's ill."

"She's always been ailing," Beau complained, his voice almost a whine. "My mother's the same way. Shouldn't coddle her. That's what my father says. You coddle a woman, she'll just get weaker. Never be useful for anything."

Papa was looking more and more disgusted, and since Beau was looking at her, he didn't notice.

"I don't want to leave Mama when she's ailing," she repeated, and took a sip of tea. "It's not decent to get married when she's sick."

"She's not sick," Beau insisted, his voice gruff. "She's just—"

"That'll be enough," Papa said, and his voice held a note that made Beau stiffen and glance at him, and then look kind of sick. Beau had gone too far, and he knew it.

"Yes, sir," Beau said. "I didn't mean any—"

"We'll forget it," Papa said, making a brushing aside motion with his hand. "But Sarah is right. She can't leave her mother while she's ailing. We'll have to talk about the wedding later."

Sarah didn't let her sigh of relief escape. She swallowed it instead and went on eating. But she was silently offering thanks. *Thank You, God. Thank You for showing me what to say. And please keep my Calvin safe. Hiram and Willie, too. And bless Minta and Bessie. Thank You again.*

seventeen

October 1860

Sarah turned from the window of the west parlor to look down at the cradle where Bessie slept. Bessie was such a good baby, either sleeping or gazing peacefully around her. That was a blessing. Because if she'd interfered with Minta's duties, Papa would have insisted that she be sent to the children's cabin where the grannies watched the other slave babies. And Minta would have been heart-broken. But they would keep Bessie in the Big House as long as they could. Every night she prayed that God would show them the way and that Bessie would continue to be such a good baby.

Sarah turned back to the window, gazing down the lane toward the road as if Calvin would be riding up it any minute now. Goodness. So much had happened in the last year. Just a year ago she and Minta had been standing in the auction house in Richmond, watching Willie being sold. They'd been so terribly afraid for him. And then Calvin had come—and she wasn't afraid anymore. As long as she had Calvin's love, she could do anything. She could refuse to marry Beau. She could even, if she had to, smuggle Bessie away to freedom and bear Papa's wrath after-wards. Loving Calvin had made her very strong. Loving Calvin—and trusting in God. That was what would keep her going until they found a way to be together, a way that would mean Minta's freedom, and Bessie's, too.

She smiled. Calvin had written to Mama that he was going to be in Richmond on Pinkerton business sometime this month. And Mama had invited him to visit. Before long they would see him again. Thank God.

Her heart beat faster at the thought, at the thought of seeing his dear face, of being able to talk to him, actually talk to him. And to touch him, just touch his hand. That he worked for Mr. Pinkerton was such a blessing. He and Willie could travel that way. Travel brought them south and allowed Calvin to be where she could see him.

Two days later, Calvin and Willie rode up the lane to the Big House. Albert opened the door with a smile. "Good afternoon, Mr. Sharp."

"Where's Minta?" Willie asked, slipping down from the horse. "I gotta see that baby! Me, I'm an uncle."

A little smile slipped across Albert's face. "Your sister's in the east parlor with Miss Sarah and Missus." He motioned to Calvin. "If you'll follow me."

Albert stopped in the doorway to the parlor. "Mr. Sharp is here, Missus."

Mrs. Hawthorne nodded and smiled. Calvin made himself smile back at her before he let himself look to Sarah. She was there in her chair, her sewing in her hands, a wide smile on her face. "Calvin!"

He knew from that one joyfully breathed word that the colonel was out of the house.

"You're here!" She dropped her needlework into her basket and hurried to him, to grasp his hands in her warm ones and gaze into his eyes. He resisted the urge to pull her into his arms and never let her go.

"It's so good to see you," she said, a faint blush tinting

her cheeks. "I've missed you."

"No more than I've missed you," he said softly. "Oh, Sarah, I—"

"Massa!" Willie cried. "Look at this here baby! Ain't she jest beautiful?"

Sarah took him by the hand and led him to the cradle. Calvin looked down. A pair of dark brown eyes gazed up at him out of a pale chocolate face. And then the little pink mouth opened in a smile and the baby cooed.

"She likes you!" Willie cried. "She knows you good!"

Calvin smiled. "I doubt that she can know that, Willie. But she can probably feel that you love her."

"Oh, I do," Willie cried. "I greatly do!"

Calvin turned to Minta. "She's a lovely baby. You must be proud."

Minta nodded. "Yes, Massa. I real proud. But Miss Sarah, she been so good to me. She helped my Bessie be borned. Without her, I wouldn't have no baby."

He might have known it. That was just like Sarah. She had such a good heart. He wasn't sure if he loved her because she was so beautiful, or so good, or just because God had meant them for each other. He turned to her. "I'm proud of you, Sarah. Really proud."

"It wasn't anything special," she said, blushing even more. "I wanted to be there. I just did what anyone would do."

Minta shook her head. "Not anyone. Miss Sarah, she stay with me all night."

Willie stuck out a finger and the baby grasped it in her little ones. "Look! She's a-hangin' on!"

Calvin nodded.

"Massa Sharp?" Minta had edged closer and reached out tentatively to touch his arm, a worried look on her face.

In surprise, he asked, "Yes, Minta? What is it?"

"I—" Her bottom lip quivered, and she clamped her mouth shut.

Sarah moved closer and put an arm around her waist. "It's just that Minta's worried about Bessie." She lowered her voice. "She's worried about Papa—about him selling—the baby."

Calvin stared at her in shock. He felt as if someone had doused him with a bucket of cold water. "The baby?" he repeated. "Sell the baby?"

Sarah nodded, her beautiful eyes gone sad. "He can, you know. He can sell her anytime he wants."

"But a baby?" he protested. "He'd sell a baby?"

Sarah nodded. "She's probably safe for another year or so. But after that, especially when she gets to be six or seven—" She swallowed hard. "Papa can sell her. And he can sell Minta before that. He can." She swallowed again and released Minta, who now had tears in her eyes. "He knows Minta helps me with Mama, but still, he might decide—"

Calvin looked down at his clenched fists. Selling a baby! How could God allow something so terrible to go on? Why didn't He do something to stop it? He sighed. He knew the answer to that—God expected *people* to stop it. People like him.

Sarah's fingers closed around his arm. "I promised Minta we wouldn't let anything like that happen. I told her if we had to, we'd send Bessie north to you. That you'd get her to Hiram." She glanced at the girl. "That's what she wants to ask you about. If you'll promise, too."

Minta nodded, her face anxious.

"Of course I'll promise," Calvin said. "When Bessie's old enough, I'll come after her myself. Maybe next spring.

She should be old enough to travel then."

Minta broke into a smile. "Thank you, Massa."

"You could come too," he said. "I think I could arrange for you both to get to Hiram."

Minta sighed, her shoulders drooping under her calico gown. "That'd be real nice, Massa. But I can't leave Miss Sarah."

"But your baby—"

"I knows," she said. "But I couldn't leave with Hiram. And I can't go with Bessie neither. I got to be here to help Miss Sarah with the runaways. Missus ain't up to it no more, her being sick so much."

"But, Minta," Sarah said, "if Bessie disappears, Papa will know you had something to do with it. He might sell *you*."

Minta shook her head. "I got to take that chance, Miss Sarah. Long as Bessie and Hiram be safe, I don't matter."

Sarah's sweet face grew determined. "Yes, you do. You matter to me. We'll have to figure out something else. I won't risk your being sold. I just won't. But don't worry." She slipped an arm through Calvin's. "I know we'll manage something. Mr. Sharp will figure it out."

Calvin swallowed a sigh. Taking a baby all the way north wouldn't be easy. But maybe Willie could think of a plan. Hiram and Brutus wouldn't have made it to Philadelphia if it hadn't been for Willie's last-minute resourcefulness.

"I'll see what I can find out," he said. "About the safest way to get Bessie north." He smiled down at Sarah and patted her hand. She smiled back at him, so he figured she'd guessed that he'd take care of Minta too. Some way or other, he'd get them to freedom. He squeezed her fingers.

"Could we go somewhere and talk?" he asked. "Just the two of us?"

Sarah sighed. "You know we can't do that. But we can sit over there. Mama will be sewing. And Minta and Willie will be busy with the baby."

"Fine," Calvin said. "I just want to sit and look at you. To touch your hand. It seems like forever, instead of just a few months."

She dimpled prettily. "I know. But I have faith in God. I believe He brought us together. And He'll see that we—" She hesitated, and another blush stained her cheeks. "I believe God wants us to be married," she said softly, but she looked directly into his eyes. "And He will show us how to do that."

"Yes," Calvin said. Sarah believed and so would he. "God will show us how."

Later that evening, Calvin took his place at the dinner table. The party was small that night, only the Hawthorne family, himself, and the Gordons. He could have done without Beau's presence, of course. Beau was so conceited, so full of himself that in other circumstances he'd have been amusing. What wasn't amusing at all was the proprietary way he ordered Sarah around, as if she were his chattel or something. *It won't always be this way,* Calvin reminded himself. *I will marry Sarah and get her away from here. I have to.*

"Is there much talk of war in Chicago?" Mr. Gordon asked through a mouthful of fried chicken.

"War?" Calvin asked, startled out of his thoughts. "War between whom?"

"Come now," the colonel said, smiling dryly. "You can't have been that busy on your business for Mr. Pinkerton. Reginald is talking about the growing conflict between the North and the South. If that reprobate Lincoln gets elected, well— You've heard what he said in '58: 'A house divided against itself cannot stand. I believe this government cannot endure permanently half slave and half free.' " He glanced at Gordon. "Here in the South we don't like the sound of that. There's been a lot of talk. The North isn't going to make us give up our way of life." His gaze probed Calvin's face. "If it tries, the Southern states might secede and set up their own government."

Calvin straightened. "I admit I've have heard some such rumors, sir," he said. "But I didn't give them much credence. I mean, we're one country, sir. How can the Southern states decide to leave?"

"We will," Gordon said, stabbing two more pieces of chicken and dropping them on his plate beside his third mound of mashed potatoes and gravy. "We don't aim to give in to the North, Mr. Sharp. Slavery is our God-given right. And we mean to keep it."

God-given, was it? But Calvin wasn't going to address *that*. He looked to the colonel. "What do *you* think, sir? Do you think it may actually come to war?"

The colonel sighed and rubbed his chin thoughtfully. "Yes, Mr. Sharp, I'm afraid it may. If Lincoln gets elected, well, we can expect trouble."

"But to split the country. . ." Calvin hesitated. "I'd be sorry to see it come to that." How could they really think they'd win a war against the North? They had few factories and—

"We got our rights!" Beau snapped, banging on the table with his fork. "No Washington politician's gonna tell us what to do." He glared around the table. "We'll fight for what's ours."

And you'll die, Calvin thought. *A war would mean so*

much killing, so much pain. But how could anyone convince these people that such a war was wrong?

Mrs. Gordon looked pale. "Beauregard," she began. "I don't want you to—"

"Of course he'll fight," Gordon declared, looking at his wife with contempt. "He's no mama's boy."

Calvin stiffened. In spite of all their pretty cavalier speeches, these Southern planters had no respect for womankind. Well, he should be fair. There must be some Southern planters who didn't treat their women like slaves or children, just as there must be some who believed slavery was wrong. He just hadn't met any of them.

"I'll fight, too, of course," Gordon said, gravy dripping from his chin. He glanced at the colonel. "So will you. We'll show—"

"No," Mrs. Hawthorne said quietly. "He won't."

Gordon looked startled. But the colonel sent his wife an affectionate glance, and said, " 'Fraid I wouldn't be much good on the battlefield these days, Reginald. The doctor says I've got a bad ticker. Got to be careful what I do."

"Well," Beau said, attacking a piece of chicken as though it meant to fight back, "we'll stand up for what's ours." He glared at Calvin. "You can just go back up North and tell 'em that. This is our country. And we don't mean to give it up."

Silence came over the room. Calvin tried to think of some way to defuse the situation, but his mind was a blank. All he could think of was men fighting and killing and dying, and all because they wanted to keep other men enslaved.

"Will you be in Virginia long, Mr. Sharp?" Mrs. Hawthorne asked finally, with a sidelong glance at Gordon.

She was obviously changing the subject. "Are you after another counterfeiter?"

"Yes, ma'am, I am," Calvin said. "Or rather I was. I've brought him to justice, and I'm on my way back to Richmond. Thought I'd stop by so Willie could see his sister."

Gordon looked up, his mouth falling open, his little eyes squinting. "You went outta your way so that a dumb pickaninny could see his sister?" he asked, his voice rising in amazement.

"Yes," Calvin said, keeping his own voice firm. He shouldn't bait the man. It wasn't sensible. It wasn't even kind. But he hated this whole wretched business. Hated it so much that sometimes he forgot he was supposed to love his enemies. So much that sometimes he didn't see why God had asked such an impossible thing of him. He swallowed and breathed a silent prayer. *I'll try, Lord. I'll try.*

"Besides, Gordon," he said, smiling at his hostess, "Mrs. Hawthorne sets the finest table in the county. I can't eat so well anywhere else." Carefully he avoided looking at Sarah. Beau might suspect that Sarah was the reason for Calvin's stopping there, but he could only suspect. And a man with a passion for food like Beau's—he might believe that food was the draw. Besides, Beau had no evidence of anything else. And Calvin didn't mean to give him any. He wanted to keep coming to Hawthorne Hill until he could figure out how to get the colonel's permission to marry Sarah. If the South did secede, if there was a war. . . But he couldn't think about that now. He'd have to trust in God. *Please, God,* he prayed, *show me how to do it. Show me how to make Sarah my wife.*

eighteen

"Miss Sarah," Minta said, turning from the window with a frown on her dark face. "Someone coming fast down the lane. Look like Mr. Beau on that red horse of his'n."

Sarah went to look for herself. Minta was right. Beau was coming—and he was coming awfully fast. She left the window and hurried to the front door. Albert was there and had it open already.

"They did it! We've seceded!" Beau cried, jumping off the horse and bounding up the steps. "Colonel, Colonel, sir! Virginia has joined the Confederacy!"

Her heart fell. Now they were really at war. She swallowed hard. She'd been hoping against hope that Virginia wouldn't secede. Her prayers hadn't been answered. She'd asked God to stop this awful war from happening. But God hadn't stopped it. Virginia had joined the Confederacy. The South would fight the North. And Calvin and Willie would be in danger. Calvin wasn't the sort of man to shirk his duty. If there was a war, he would fight. She felt a faintness creeping over her. *Please, God, keep Calvin safe.*

She turned away from the door. She had to tell Mama.

A few minutes later, Beau strode into the east parlor where Mama lay weakly on the chaise. Sarah sat beside her, the hartshorn in her hand in case they needed it again. "Here you are," he said, his voice accusing.

"Please, Beau." Sarah gave him a pleading look. She'd just gotten Mama calmed down and now here was Beau, ready to upset her again. "Mama's not feeling well today. And this news is very disturbing."

Beau threw himself into a chair and stretched out his muddy boots. "Sarah, we've got to talk."

She motioned to Minta and handed her the hartshorn. Then she turned to face him. "Talk about what, Beau? I don't want to hear any more about a war or fighting. Neither does Mama."

"This ain't about fighting," Beau said. He straightened in the chair. "We've got to get married now. Surely you can see that."

Her heart jumped up into her throat. Did he never think of anything else? He was so persistent. But she wasn't going to give in. Not now. "No, I don't see it."

He jumped to his feet and stood glaring down at her. "Sarah! I'm sick and tired of your putting off our wedding! You've been doing it for months now—and it's got to stop!"

"Have you spoken to Papa about it?" she asked.

There was a moment's hesitation, then he said, "He agrees with me. He thinks we—"

"I believe I can speak for myself, Beau." Papa came slowly into the room and settled into a chair near Mama.

Sarah didn't like the grayness in his face or the way he eased himself down in the chair. These days he wasn't looking at all well.

"Now," Papa said, looking at her, "I suppose Beau wants you to set a date for the wedding."

"Yes, Pa—"

"I do!" Beau said. "We've been putting it off too long. Sarah's going to be my wife. She might as well be my wife now." He grinned. "Maybe we can even start our family before I go off to fight."

Papa looked back to her, his forehead wrinkling in a frown. "What do you think, Sarah?"

It wasn't often he asked her opinion, but she knew that in his own way Papa loved her. What should she say? She couldn't tell anything about his thoughts from his expression. But surely if he meant to insist on their marriage, he would just have agreed with Beau. She struggled to keep her fear off her face. She didn't want to be in the family way from Beau. She didn't want Beau to touch her. But she couldn't tell Papa that. *Steady,* she told herself. *God will help you.* She took a deep breath. "I know Beau's been waiting a while, Papa. But I think it would be selfish to be thinking of ourselves at a time like this. When the Confederacy is at risk, we should put all our efforts into saving it." She glanced at Mama. "And Mama is ill, you know. I don't want to leave her."

Beau was glowering now, glaring from her to Mama and back again. She risked a glance at Papa. He didn't look happy about any of this. And that awful look of grayness about his eyes—

"Colonel," Beau said, his voice rising, "I insist that—"

Papa straightened, and his old look of command returned. "Beauregard Gordon! This is my home and Sarah is my daughter. You don't insist on anything!"

"Yes, sir. Sorry, sir." Beau looked genuinely crestfallen, but that didn't stop him from going on. "But I've been waiting for a real long time, Colonel. You know that. And I thought with me going off to war and all. . . Well, it just seemed like we ought to be married first."

Papa nodded. "I can see your point, Beau. But I think Sarah has a point, too." He sighed. "She's still very young. Besides, the fighting should be over soon, and then you can have a proper wedding, with everything that goes with it." He sighed again and rubbed his left arm. "I don't want Sarah to be left a widow. Nor to have a child while you're away at war and her mother's ill. So, right now, I think you'd better wait. When the war is over, that'll be time enough to—"

Beau's face turned red. "But—"

"I said you'd better wait," Papa repeated, his voice growing harsher. "And that's what I meant."

Beau gulped in air. "Yes, sir."

Slowly, carefully, Sarah let out her breath. *Thank You, God,* she breathed. *Thank You. Please keep Calvin safe. And Hiram and Willie. And Beau, too.* As horrible as he was, she didn't want anything bad to happen to Beau.

"Then I'm going to Richmond tomorrow," Beau snapped.

He turned toward the door. "But I'll be back. And next summer when this war is over, we'll be married. I promise."

She didn't reply to that. She couldn't.

"Sarah," Mama breathed, her voice quivering.

Sarah turned back to her. "Yes, Mama?"

"Help me to my room, dear. I need to lie down."

"Yes, Mama." She took Mama's hand and helped her to her feet.

"Good-bye, Beau," Mama said. "God be with you."

"Thank you, Mrs. Hawthorne," Beau had the grace to say. "I hope you get to feeling better."

Well, that was a surprise! Until now, Beau had never admitted that Mama could be sick. "I'll wait 'til you come back," Beau said to Sarah, his voice truculent. "I want a proper good-bye."

"Yes, Beau." She could give him that much. After all, he was going off to war.

After she had Mama settled on the chaise in her room, Sarah kissed her cheek and said, "I guess I'd better go. Beau is waiting."

Mama raised a hand to catch hers. "You were wise, my dear. Don't make Beau any promises, but be kind to him. He is going to fight a war."

Sarah shuddered. "I know, Mama." She swallowed over the lump in throat. "Do you think Calvin will be fighting too?"

"I don't know," Mama said, sighing. "We can only trust that God will help us through these troubling times."

"Yes, Mama." Sarah turned to the door. "I'll be back in a little while."

Beau was pacing in the foyer when she came down.

"Where's Papa?" she asked. "He was looking awfully pale."

Beau shrugged. "It's big news—this war thing. He's just excited."

She swallowed the sharp words that came to her tongue. There was no point in arguing with him. Beau seldom saw anything he didn't want to see.

"Are you going to leave tomorrow?" she asked, stopping in front of him.

"Unless you give me a reason to stay." He leaned toward her.

She managed not to back away. "I can't do that, Beau. You heard what Papa said. And he's right."

Beau's gaze probed her face. "You sure there's no other reason?"

Her heart threatened to jump right out of her mouth. Had he guessed about Calvin? "I don't want to have a baby now, Beau. Mama needs me. Besides," she forced herself to smile at him. "I'll be enough worried about you as it is."

He smiled back at her. "No need to worry," he said. " 'Cause I'm coming back. I'm coming back—and I'm going to marry you." And he kissed her.

She didn't move away or try to stop him. But she couldn't bring herself to kiss him back. Beau's kiss was so different from Calvin's—it was like a whole different thing.

When Beau released her, he stood looking down at her, puzzlement in his eyes. She guessed he'd kissed a lot of girls, and most of them had responded more than she had. "You are young," he said then. "Maybe your Papa's right. But we'll get married soon enough. This war'll be over by fall. We're gonna show those Yankees that they can't push us around." He grinned. "And then I'll be back. We'll get married and have ourselves a house full of babies."

He gave her another quick kiss and then turned away. "Bye for now."

nineteen

May 1863

Sarah put the wildflowers down by the wooden cross that marked the grave and turned away, tears in her eyes. With the war still raging on, there was no chance of getting a proper headstone. It was hard to believe that Papa was gone. Sometimes he had been unkind to the slaves, but he had loved her and Mama, and she and Mama had loved him. It hardly seemed possible that he was gone. But he was. Mr. Lincoln's Emancipation Proclamation had freed the slaves, at least those in Confederate territory, but it seemed to have hastened Papa's death.

He hadn't been well before that, of course. The pallor she'd seen on his face the day Beau told them Virginia had seceded had grown day by day. His steps had faltered and slowed, his breathing grown harder and harder. It was painful to see him dying like that right in front of them, painful for Mama, too. But there was nothing they could do for him.

One afternoon that last week Papa had called her to his bedside. "I'm afraid we're going to lose this war," he whispered. "Take care of your mother."

"Oh, Papa."

"Don't cry, my dear." He patted her hand. "I've made my peace with God. I'm ready to go."

She wondered if part of that peace had been refusing to

make her marry Beau, but she didn't ask. She hoped that Papa was really with God. Some days, thinking of the misery slavery had caused, she couldn't conceive how any slaveholder would ever make it to heaven. But of course that wasn't up to her. Who was saved and who wasn't— that was God's business. Not up to any person. That was probably a lucky thing.

Before she had come to the grave, she'd gone up to the hollow tree in the woods, the one she and Calvin used for a mail place. Since the war had been going on so long, it was hard to get letters through in the regular way. So he sent letters to her, unsigned, carried by people traveling through. And she left hers there for someone to carry back to him. But sometimes she didn't hear anything for months. And today there had been nothing there.

Sarah slipped her hand into the pocket of her skirt and touched Calvin's last letter, worn from many readings. Just touching it gave her strength. It had been so long since she'd seen him. And when she had, it was just for a stolen hour or two, hiding in Minta's cabin or the woods so Papa wouldn't know Calvin was there. Afraid even to laugh in case Vickers might hear them.

She counted back. Six months since Calvin had been there last. Papa had still been alive then. They'd known, though, what was coming. And Calvin had held her close and told her not to worry, that someday the war would be over. He had promised her that after the war, God willing, they would be husband and wife.

She'd cherished that hope, especially when Beau came home wounded to captain the local regiment and started in again about their being married. Mama had put a stop to that, finally, by telling him he was insulting Papa's memory and that she didn't want to hear any more about a wedding until the war was over.

Sarah turned toward the house. It was time to get back to Mama. It would be suppertime soon. Minta would have something cooked. She could do wonders with wild plants out of the woods and fields, but she had her hands full with Bessie. Bessie was almost two and determined to touch everything within touching distance, and some things that weren't.

Sarah smiled. At least Bessie could stay with her mama; she didn't have to go to the children's cabin. But to think that Hiram had never seen his daughter—that was sad.

Her fingers touched the letter again. Hiram had come back from Canada to serve with the Union Army, one of Calvin's letters had said. But that had been months ago, and there had been no word of him since then.

Please God, keep him safe. And keep my Calvin safe, please. I don't feel right about him doing what he does. But he had to make the decision that was right for him. He told me how he promised You that he'd do everything in his power to end slavery. And when Mr. Pinkerton asked him to collect information on Southern troops, he decided that was the best way he could help. She sighed. *Dear God, I don't know if it's right or wrong. I just know I love him. Please keep him safe.*

She turned toward the house.

"Hist!"

The sound came from the bushes to her left. She stopped and listened. Nothing. She started on again.

"Hist! Miss Sarah."

That sounded like—her heart pounded. It sounded like Willie! She stopped again.

"Minta's cabin," the voice said.

Sarah didn't question. Heart pounding, knees shaking
she turned down the path toward Slave Row. She wanted to
run. If Calvin was waiting for her in Minta's cabin. .
Walk, she told herself sternly. *Don't run. And don't look
happy. You're just to check on someone—on Lucy'
girl, maybe. Or to see how the grannies are doing in the
children's cabin. Yes, that's what you'll tell Vickers if you
see him. You have every right to be here.*

The sun was going down, and the inside of Minta'
cabin was dark with shadows. She slipped through the
door and looked around. He was standing by the cold
hearth, his back to the door. A stray beam of sunshine
peeping through the paneless window illumined that part
of the cabin, letting her see that his shoulders drooped and
he'd lost weight. His clothes, nondescript clothes, hung on
him. She knew he had to pretend to be a civilian, and if he
got caught he could be hanged. The thought had given her
nightmares. Now it sent her hurrying across the packed
dirt floor.

"Calvin! I'm here."

He turned, joy lighting his face. "Sarah! Oh, Sarah!" And
he opened his arms.

She went right into them. He was there. He was really
there—and he was alive. That was all that mattered now.

"I've missed you so much," he said, gazing down into
her eyes. "Are you all right?"

"Yes." She swallowed over her tears. "Papa's gone. He
died in January."

"Yes," Calvin said. "I expected that."

"I think he was sorry," she said. "At the end he said he'
made his peace with God." She looked up at him. "Do you

ink he could? Do you think God could forgive him?"

Calvin kissed her forehead. "God can forgive anything," e said. "God can forgive anyone."

"Thank you," she said, burrowing into his arms. "I needed hear that."

"How's your mother?"

"She's getting weaker. She's always been sickly. But los-g Papa—she loved him, you know. In spite of—"

"I know," Calvin said gently, hugging her. "And Minta d the baby?"

"They're both well. As well as anyone can be in this wful war." She looked around. "Minta doesn't sleep here aymore. After Papa died, we asked her to sleep in the Big ouse. Her and Bessie. It's safer."

"Yes." He held her off at arm's length. "How are you? ou look so thin."

"I'm all right," she said. "But I've missed you so much. alvin, when will this awful war be over?"

He smoothed her hair. "I don't know, dear. I just don't now. No one thought it would last this long."

She sighed. "Sometimes I think it will go on forever and rever."

He chuckled weakly. "I know. Sometimes I think so, too. ut it won't. The South can't hold out forever. We *will* win."

She looked around again. "Where's Willie?"

"He went to look for Minta and Bessie."

"But if Vickers sees him!"

Calvin shook his head. "Vickers hasn't seen him for two ars, Sarah. These last months Willie has shot up like a eed. You'll hardly know him yourself."

Sarah sighed against his chest. "How long can you stay is time?"

Calvin looked around. "Do you suppose we'd be safe i̶ here tonight?"

She looked up in surprise.

"We haven't slept in several days," he explained. "I'r̶ afraid we'll fall off our horses."

"Where are they?"

"Willie hid them in the woods. He has a place there."

"I'm afraid you can't stay here," she said. "Vickers migh̶ find you."

He sighed. "I guess we'll ride on."

"No," she said. "Wait 'til it gets dark and then come u̶ to the house."

"Sarah." His eyes shone with his love. "I don't want ̶ put you in danger."

"You won't," she said. "Please. There's only Minta ar̶ Bessie in the house after dark. Albert left after Papa died— said he wasn't going to be a slave anymore. And Coc̶ goes to her cabin before dark. There's no one else in th̶ house. You can sneak in and sleep in a bed."

The sigh that trembled through him shook his who̶ body. "A bed," he said, as if it were unimaginable. "I haven̶ slept in a bed for so long."

"Then do it," she said. "Wait about half an hour afte̶ dark and then come up to the house. I'll leave the bac̶ door unlocked. You can sleep in a bed and be up and awa̶ before daybreak."

"I shouldn't," he said. "But I can't resist." He gathered h̶ close for one last kiss. "I love you, Sarah Hawthorne. No̶ you'd better go take care of your mother. I'll see you later.'

She hesitated and he smiled and said, "I promise. No̶ go."

She reached up and kissed him once more lightly on th̶

ips, and then, afraid to look back, she slipped out the door
and hurried toward the house. Her heart was singing, but
she kept her mouth in a sober line. Anyone seeing her
would just think she was hurrying to the Big House to take
care of Mama.

&

"Massa!"

Calvin came instantly awake. Their months on the road
had taught him to sleep lightly. "What is it?"

"Joe come to the back door," Willie whispered. "Vickers
give him a message to take to Mr. Beau."

Evidently, fear had made Willie forget to speak properly.
"Beau!" Calvin said. "Why should Vickers send Beau a
message in the middle of the night?"

Willie moved closer. "Vickers send Joe with a letter. Joe
come to me to read it. It say Vickers think someone here
who shouldn't be—you. And he tell Mr. Beau to come in
the night and catch you."

Calvin reached for his clothes. "Why did Joe bring this
letter to you?"

Willie squirmed. "I seen Joe this afternoon. Didn't think
I'd do no harm. Vickers was drunk in his cabin. I–I told
Joe I could read."

Calvin buttoned his shirt and pulled on his trousers. "So
he brought you the letter to read."

"Yes. He suspecting something. He say Mr. Beau sniff-
ing round here a lot since the colonel gone. Mr. Beau
wanting to marry Miss Sarah, but Missus say no."

Willie shook his head. "Nobody want Mr. Beau for a
massa. He too hard a man. But he don't give up easy. He
used to getting his own way."

"How long have we got?" Calvin asked.

"The note say to come 'round midnight," Willie said. "I eleven now."

Calvin pulled on his boots. At least he'd had a coupl hours of sleep. "We'll leave right away," he said.

Willie nodded. "What about Miss Sarah—?"

"Show me her room," Calvin said. "I have to tell he good-bye."

"Yes, Massa."

Calvin made up the bed, then scrutinized the room, mak ing sure there was no sign of his occupancy. Satisfied, h said, "Let's go."

It took only minutes to rouse Sarah and tell her what wa going on. He gave her one quick kiss and said, "I'll b back when I can. I love you."

"I love you, too," Sarah said, her chin set bravely. "I' be waiting for you."

Sarah went back to her bedroom and took the packet o Calvin's letters from the bureau to hide them under th mattress. Then she climbed into bed and waited. At mid night Beau arrived, surrounding the house with Souther troops and pounding on the front door. She took her tim getting to it, making sure her hair was down and rumple and her robe carefully tied.

"What on earth is it?" she asked, opening the door an rubbing at her eyes. "Beau? What are you doing here? It the middle of the night."

Beau's face was grim. "I'm looking for him."

"For who?" she asked. There was no need for her to pre tend to be irritated. She was. "What on earth are you tall ing about?"

"I'm talking about that Yankee!" Beau roared. "He's hi ing in here."

"Beauregard Gordon," she warned. "Kindly lower your voice. Mama's sleeping."

He didn't even look sheepish. "I doubt that," he said. "Now, I'm going to search this house. Every last inch of it. And they're searching Slave Row, too."

She shrugged. "Waste your time if you want to. I'm telling you, there's no one here." She turned toward the stairs. "I'm going up to tell Mama what's going on. All this noise will have her worried."

"I'm coming with you," Beau said, his voice threatening.

"Do whatever you like," she said. "I'm going up to Mama."

Beau followed her. In spite of Mama's scornful looks, he searched her room from top to bottom, even to looking under the bed and in the wardrobe.

Then he turned to Sarah. "You come with me," he said. "I don't want you warning him." He looked at Minta, who was clutching a wide-eyed Bessie. "She can stay with your mama."

Sarah started to protest, but Mama said, "It's all right, Sarah. Go with the man. We know he's not going to find anything. Maybe then we can finally get back to sleep."

So Sarah trailed Beau from room to room while he practically tore the place apart. *Thank You, God,* she breathed as Beau searched the room where an hour before Calvin had been sleeping. *Thank You for warning us.*

Finally, after he'd been through every room, Beau gave up. She followed him down the front staircase. He turned to her. "I'm sorry for the inconvenience," he said, trying to smile. "But we had a report that a Yankee was in here, and we had to check it out."

"A report?" she asked, trying to sound inquisitive, and

nothing else. "A report from whom?"

"From Vickers," Beau said, his look sheepish.

She managed a laugh. "Vickers? Are you sure it wasn't [a] bottle he saw this Yankee in? You know how Vickers [is] about his liquor."

Beau glared at her. "You ain't supposed to know abou[t] such things," he said. "Ladies don't."

She shrugged. "I can hardly help it," she said. "Vicker[s] is drunk most of the time now, since Papa died."

"That's why you need—" He stopped abruptly, obvi ously deciding this wasn't the time to press the marriag[e] issue. "Lock this door after me," he said. "And don't l[et] anyone in."

"I won't," she said. "I certainly won't."

And finally he was gone. He was gone, and Calvin wa[s] safely away. Bless the day that Willie had learned to rea[d.] Bless the day that Calvin had come into her life. *Than[k] You, God,* she breathed again. *Thank You.*

twenty

July 1863

The darkness of night had fallen. Sarah turned from making Mama comfortable or at least as comfortable as she could in this heat.

"Go to bed," Mama said. "There's nothing more you can do for me, dear."

"Yes, Mama." Sarah kissed her cheek. "Good night." She turned to Minta. "Call me if you need me."

"Yes, Miss Sarah."

It was Minta's night to stay with Mama. They took turns now.

They had put Bessie in a room of her own, close by, but where she could sleep undisturbed.

Thank God for Bessie, Sarah thought as she went down the hall and into the room she and Minta shared. She stepped out of her gown and pulled on her nightdress. Little Bessie made life bearable for them all. She didn't know there was a war. She only knew that there was a great world waiting for her to explore. And she explored it with such joy, her dark eyes wide, her little mouth turned up in a smile.

Sarah knelt beside the bed to say her prayers. No matter how exhausted she was, she never went to bed without saying her prayers. *Please, God,* she prayed now. *Help us through this bad time. Help Mama and keep Calvin safe.*

Minta and Bessie. Hiram and Willie, too. Thank You.

Wearily she climbed into the bed. Tomorrow would be another long day, a day without Calvin. But there would be a lot to do. She closed her eyes.

She was just dozing off, floating in a wonderful world where Mama was well, Sarah's stomach was full, and she could see Calvin's smile, when the door opened.

"Sarah. Sarah, wake up."

She sat up. "Calvin?" And then she laughed at herself. She was still sleeping, dreaming of him because she loved him so much. She started to lie back down.

"Sarah."

"Calvin, is it really you?"

He stood just inside the door. "Yes, Sarah. It's really me. Dress please, and come out to me."

"Yes, yes, of course. Right away."

He closed the door and she rushed into her clothes, her fingers trembling with excitement. *Calvin, here.* How long could he stay?

Minutes later, she opened the door. Calvin was sitting on the floor, his back against the wall. He got to his feet and came toward her. She went right into his arms. "Oh, Calvin is it safe for you to be here? You know Beau watches this place."

"I know," he said. "But I had to come. There's someone with me. An escaped prisoner. I'm taking him north with me."

Her heart almost stood still. "An escaped—"

"Yes," Calvin said. "I'm helping him get home."

"But if you're caught—"

He shrugged. "If I'm caught, I'm dead anyway. He knows the risk, and he's willing. He's a minister, Sarah. He can marry us."

"Marry?" she said. Her knees threatened to give way and she clung to him. Maybe she was still dreaming.

"Yes." He took her hand. "Come on; he's waiting in your mother's room."

She had to laugh. No man but Papa had ever set foot in Mama's room. And now there was a stranger there. It was all so improper. But the war had changed everything. No one cared about improper now.

Willie stepped forward, Minta beside him. They were both grinning. "Mr. Sharp got word from Hiram," Minta said. "He been shot, but he gonna be all right."

"Oh, Minta. Thank God."

Calvin slipped an arm around Sarah's waist and led her to the bed where Mama lay propped up against the pillows. "Mrs. Hawthorne," he said. "I'm asking your permission to marry your daughter. I love her. I'll always love her."

"I know," Mama said. "I know you do." She looked at Sarah with a weak smile. "And she loves you. I know that, too. You have my permission to marry."

Calvin motioned and out of the shadows by the door a man came. His clothes were tattered and torn, and his face was lined and weary. But his eyes were serene, speaking of great faith. In his hands he held Mama's Bible.

Calvin took her trembling hand in his. "Will you marry me, Sarah? Now, tonight?"

"Oh yes, Calvin. Yes."

"Good."

His arm tightened around her waist. "We can't stay," he said. "I've got information the Union Army needs. And I want to get Burt over the Union lines as soon as I can. But he said he'd do this for me. For us." He looked down at her. "We can wait if you want to, but—"

"No. No; I don't want to wait." She turned to the minis ter. "Please, go on, Mr.—Burt. I want to be Calvin's wife."

Half an hour later Sarah stood in the shadow of the dark ened back door and watched them creep away—Willie, th minister, and Calvin, her husband. Her *husband*. The wor sang in her heart. She was Calvin's wife. She had no ring no marriage lines, not even a wedding night. But she wa well and truly married, married in the sight of God. A long last.

"Miss Sarah," Minta said from behind her. "Your mam wanting to talk to you."

"I'm coming," Sarah said, shutting the door and pullin the bolt home. She turned toward the stairs.

"Tell me again what Calvin said about Hiram. I was s excited I'm not sure I got it all."

"Mr. Sharp say he ask about Hiram," Minta said, he eyes bright. "He ask them big men he know—in Washing ton. They found out Hiram been shot. Got hit in his arm."

"Oh, Minta, I'm sorry."

"No need, Miss Sarah. Hiram alive, and he can walk That all I care 'bout. Maybe he be coming home soon. pray so."

"Me, too," Sarah said.

They had reached Mama's room and they went in to he "Sarah," Mama said. "I hope we have done the righ thing."

Sarah perched on the side of the big bed. "Of course w did, Mama. I love Calvin and he loves me."

"I know that," Mama said. "But you know the onl reason we've been safe here, two white women alone, because of Beau. He's made sure no soldiers bothered us."

"I know, Mama."

"And maybe you'd have been safer marrying him."

"No!"

"I know you don't love him. But if this war goes on much longer, there's no telling what will happen."

"I don't care," Sarah said, taking Mama's fingers in her own. "I would never be Beau's wife, no matter what." She shuddered. "I couldn't. Not while I love Calvin."

"Then we did right," Mama said. "Go to bed, dear. You need your rest."

"Yes, Mama." She turned to Minta. "I'll look in on Bessie as I go."

"Thank you," Minta said, and plumped up Mama's pillows.

Sarah eased open Bessie's door and stepped in to stand beside the crib. Moonlight shone through the lace curtains, making a little patch of light where Bessie lay, curled up on her side, one thumb in her mouth. Sarah smiled. Maybe someday she'd have a baby. Someday when this war was over and the world returned to sanity.

She crept back out, easing the door shut, and went on down the hall to her room. Maybe she'd dream of Calvin tonight. She did most nights. But tonight was different. Tonight she was Calvin's wife.

❧

"Miss Sarah. Miss Sarah, you got to come."

Sarah came awake, out of a beautiful dream of Calvin. She sat up. "Minta, what is it?"

"The Missus, Miss Sarah. She doing poorly. She say to come get you."

Her hands trembling, Sarah pulled on her robe and hurried down the hall. "Mama, what is it?"

"It's. . .time," Mama said.

"Time for what?" Sarah asked, still half asleep.

"I'm going. . .home," Mama said. "The angels. . .are coming. . .for me."

"Mama! No!"

"Yes," Mama breathed. "But first. . .you have. . .to know."

"Know what?" Sarah asked. She didn't want to hear any of this. She couldn't lose Mama. She just couldn't. *Please, God,* she prayed. *Not tonight, please.*

"Minta and you," Mama said, her voice so soft Sarah could hardly hear it. "You. . .are. . .sisters."

Sarah thought she'd heard wrong until Minta whispered, "Sisters, Missus?"

"Yes," Mama breathed. "The colonel. . .was Minta's. . . father. Her mother. . .was my maid. He sent. . .her away. . . after I. . .found out."

"Mama, I—"

"You don't need to say anything," Mama said, seeming to find some extra strength inside herself. She pressed Sarah's hand. "You and Minta, you take care of each other. And of Bessie."

"Yes, Mama," Sarah said, swallowing her tears. She reached for Minta's hand.

"Yes, Missus. We take care of each other. I promise," Minta said, taking Mama's other hand.

"I promise, too, Mama."

"Good." The word came out like a sigh of relief. "Kiss me, Sarah."

Sarah bent and touched her lips to Mama's withered cheek. "I love you, Mama."

"I love you, too," Mama said. "Don't grieve for me, child. I'm going home. I'll be happy there." And she closed her eyes.

Sarah stood there for an endless minute, listening as

Mama's breath came and went, came and went. And then there was silence in the room. Terrible, loud silence.

"She gone, Miss Sarah," Minta said. "She gone home." And they fell, crying, into each other's arms.

twenty-one

End of March 1865

The sun was sinking as Sarah put the wildflowers on Mama's grave. She knelt there, before the two crosses, in her dirty, torn dress.

This war had gone on so long. It seemed that it would never ever end. Her stomach rumbled. She was hungry, but these days she was always hungry. They all were. Bessie, and Minta, and the other slave women who'd stayed on the plantation after the men came one by one and asked permission to go fight for freedom. The women stayed because the Hill was the only home they and their children had ever known. Sarah did what she could to care for them, but they were all forever hungry. Maybe tomorrow she'd take the children and look for some wild dandelions. Then they could have some greens for supper. At least it was spring and things would be growing again, wild things, anyway. The Yankees didn't usually bother burning them as they'd been burning whatever crops the women managed to sow. The animals were all gone, of course. There probably wasn't a farm animal or bird within a hundred miles of the Yankee line.

Since Sherman had marched through Georgia last winter, burning everything in his way, most Yankees seemed to think that destroying everything was the best way to end the war. It might be. She didn't know. She only knew that she was hungry, had been hungry for so long that she couldn't remember what it was like to be full. And she was just as afraid of Yankees as she was of Confederates, maybe even more afraid since to the Yankees *she* was the enemy. But at least Vickers had left the day after Beau had made all that fuss about searching for Calvin, and they hadn't seen him in the months since. Thank God for that.

She turned back toward the Row. They'd moved into Minta's cabin the spring after Mama's death—she and Minta and Bessie. It seemed safer there than in the Big House. The slave women accepted her and cared for her as they cared for each other, sharing whatever they could find to eat. And she and Minta had grown even closer. She'd told Minta to forget the *Miss* and just call her Sarah—they were sisters after all. Bessie called her Auntie and treated her as she treated the others.

Now Sarah went to the dead tree herself to look for Calvin's letters. She went every day, sometimes twice a day. But lately there hadn't been any to add to those she kept in the tin box in the hidey-hole under the mattress boards. Letters didn't come often, but she tried not to worry. She did know that Calvin had gotten Burt the minister safely through, and Burt was back with his grateful wife and family. And word had come that Hiram was recovered from his wound and gone back to the Union Army to fight some more for freedom. Calvin had even written that there was talk in the Union forces that this spring or summer would see the end of fighting. How she prayed to God that was true.

But Beau couldn't see an end to anything. At least, not an end that meant the Yankees had gotten their way. He was still sure the Confederacy would win, that slavery would prevail. And, of course, he'd objected strenuously to her moving into the cabin with Minta. But she'd told him it was none of his business. This was her land, and she'd do as she pleased on it. He still hung around, but he seemed to have realized, finally, that he wouldn't get anywhere by bullying her.

As the darkness fell around them, she shared a bowl of thin soup with the others, and then, in the darkness, the women and children went to their cabins. They lit no fires at night now, feeling it safer to lie huddled in the darkness, showing no lights that might bring Yankee soldiers their way.

She and Minta and Bessie shared the cornhusk mattress and the gourd quilt that had been Minta's pride and joy. They'd brought the comforters from the Big House. And everything else they thought they could use. The winter had been cold.

She and Minta and Bessie knelt on the earthen floor beside the cornhusk mattress that was now their bed. "Dear Lord Jesus," Minta prayed aloud as they often did now. "Please keep our Hiram safe, and Willie and Mr. Calvin, and all them that's fighting to bring us freedom. And help us stay safe 'til this war be over. And bless Sarah and my Bessie."

"Bless my daddy," Bessie said, as she had every night of her life since she could say the words. "And bless my mama, and my auntie Sarah. And my uncle Willie, and my uncle Calvin. And all them that needs it."

Sarah smiled in the darkness. Trust Bessie to think of everyone. Bessie had never known any life but this one, and she was still the most cheerful and happy little girl. A blessing to them all—like the other children.

"Dear God," Sarah said. "Thank You for keeping us together. Thank You that we have each other to see us through this time. Please bless Calvin and Hiram and Willie, and Minta and Bessie. Amen."

"Amen," Minta and Bessie echoed. And then still in their day clothes, they settled onto the mattress, Bessie wiggling in between them. They slept in their clothes now, in case soldiers came around.

Lying there in the darkness, Sarah thought of Calvin, as she did every night. They'd been married almost two years. And they'd never spent a night together, never really been man and wife. She'd asked him about it when he came back the first time after their wedding. But, though he'd held her close and even kissed her, he'd refused to go any further, saying that he couldn't bear to think of her being with child and him not there to care for her. And because she loved him, she'd agreed to wait 'til the war was over. And she hadn't told him that she was afraid, afraid something would happen to him and she'd never get the chance to know all of his love. Afraid she'd never get to be a wife at all, then, because she'd never love another man. But she kept all those thoughts sealed in her heart, not bothering him with them. She just told him she loved him, praying to God to keep her strong.

Please, God, she prayed, *please help us all.*

Someone was shaking her, but she didn't want to wake up. She was so tired, too tired. She tried to go back to sleep, but the shaking went on.

"Sarah, wake up!"

She forced herself to consciousness. Minta was staring down at her, her eyes wide. "Minta, what is it?"

"A boy come from Mr. Beau's," Minta said, her voice

quivering. "Yankees been there. They shot Mr. Beau. He dead."

"Oh, no!" Beau didn't deserve that.

"They burn his house down," Minta went on. "And when his mama try to stop 'em, they shoot her. Boy say she dead too. And then they burn Slave Row, not a cabin left a-standin' there."

Tears welled up in Sarah's eyes. Poor Mrs. Gordon. Beau and that house were all she'd had since Mr. Gordon had been killed at Manassas.

"You're sure she's dead?" Sarah asked. "There's nothing we can do?"

"Nothing," Minta said, her teeth chattering. "But there more. Boy say Yankees coming this way. Gonna burn the Big House and our Slave Row. They drunk, he say. They burn everything in sight."

"The women!" Sarah cried. "We've got to get the women and children out of the cabins. Tell them to hide in the woods and—"

"Sarah, I got an idea. We need our cabins. Maybe—maybe I kin save 'em. And you."

"Me?" A cold shiver slithered down her back.

"Boy say them soldiers so drunk they was gonna use Mrs. Gordon, to—you know. 'Til she get crazylike. Iffen they see you, we can't stop 'em."

"I'll go off in the woods and—"

Minta grabbed her by the shoulders. "You trust me?"

What a question. "Of course, I trust you. I trust you with my life."

"Then here's what I think we oughta do."

Sarah clutched the tin box that held Calvin's precious letters and inched one leg into a more comfortable position.

If only she could stop shivering. Minta had put one of the quilts over her and the earth around her wasn't that cold. The boards and cornhusk mattress kept out the night air. But she was cold inside, cold at the thought of what drunken Yankee soldiers wanted to do to her. *Think of something else. Think of the slaves who've lain here. They were scared, too. But they trusted in God.*

She could smell the slightly bitter musty scent of the earth around her. So many slaves had hidden in this place—they'd never kept track, but she knew there'd been a lot—holding their breaths for fear of discovery, for fear they'd be sent back to slavery. *Please, God,* she prayed. *Make Minta's plan work. Please.*

Above her the cornhusk mattress rustled. Bessie whispered, "Don't you worry none, Auntie. I do 'xactly like Mama say."

It was a crazy plan, but it was all they had. She would trust in God and wait.

Because she was in the earth, she heard the vibrations of the hooves a long way off. The Yankees were coming. And then the hooves stopped, and she knew they were there, Yankee soldiers in front of the Big House. There was nothing to see there in the darkness of the hidey-hole, but she kept her eyes open, staring as though she could see the scene at the Big House.

Minta confronting the Yankee soldiers, asking, no—begging—for the privilege of burning down the Big House that now stood deserted. The other women screaming and begging for torches, too. Would Minta be able to convince the Yankees that they hated the master and mistress who'd run away? Would she be able to save Slave Row?

Even covered as she was, Sarah could hear the shouts

and screams of the women as they milled about the Yankee soldiers. Her legs twitched. She wanted to run, far away from here. But she had to lie still, to trust in God. *The Lord is my Shepherd.*

She heard the soldier's footsteps before he reached the door. So did Bessie. "I want my mama!" she wailed, just like she'd been told, thrashing around on the cornhusk mattress. "I sick. I so sick! Where my mama?"

Sarah held her breath. *Please, God. Please.*

There was a long silence. Then, "Easy, little girl," the soldier said. "She'll be back."

"I want my mama!" Bessie repeated and started to sob in earnest.

After another minute or so the soldier left, mumbling, "Don't cry. She'll be back."

Sarah knew when he left because Bessie's crying eased off. "He gone," she whispered finally. "But I do want my mama. I hope she come soon."

The minutes passed, oh, so slowly. The shouting and screaming went on. And Sarah lay there, clutching Calvin's letters, waiting.

"They burning it," Bessie cried, bouncing up on the mattress. "They burning the Big House! I see the fire! I so scared! I want my mama!" The mattress rustled above Sarah's head. Terror grabbed at her heart.

"Bessie! Bessie!" She couldn't let Bessie leave the cabin. A four-year-old wouldn't be safe out there. "Bessie, listen. Remember, Mama said to stay here."

"But, Auntie, I so scared!"

"I know," Sarah whispered. "Lie down. Put your head near the edge of the mattress. Up here near mine. Let' say the Bible words together. But if you hear someone

coming, tell me, so I can stop. Will you say the Bible words
with me?"

Bessie's voice quivered, but she said, "Yes, Auntie, I
say 'em."

So they repeated the words together, " 'The LORD is my
shepherd; I shall not want. . .he leadeth me beside the still
waters. He restoreth my soul.' "

They went through the Twenty-third Psalm. Once, twice.
They went on for what seemed like an endless time. Her
mouth grew dry as dust, but Sarah didn't dare stop. She
had to keep Bessie in the cabin.

Finally, Bessie said, "Someone coming! I hear someone
coming!" Sarah fell silent, her heart pounding, her hands
clutching the tin box.

"Mama!" Bessie screamed with joy. "Mama, you come
back!"

Sarah let out a sigh of relief. *Thank You, God.*

"Yes," Minta said, breathing heavily. "You done good.
A soldier come and tol' me you was sick. He tol' me they
wouldn't burn the cabins counta you. You done good,
chil'. Now, we got to get your auntie out from under
them boards."

The boards came away and Sarah pulled in a deep breath
of the night air, night air laden with the smell of burning.
She sat up. "The others? Minta, is *everyone* all right?"

"Didn't no one get hurt," Minta said. " 'Cepting our
throats hurt from screaming."

Sarah climbed out of the hole. "And the little ones?"

"They all stayed with the grannies. We all all right."

"Thanks to you," Sarah said. "Your plan worked."

"Praise the Lord Jesus," Minta breathed. "I never been
so scared in my life. Even of ole Vickers. But we went

running and screaming, and we told them Yankees how we
wanted to burn the place ourselves. And they laughed and
give us the torches." She looked down, tears in her eyes. "
sorry, Miss Sarah, sorry 'bout the Big House. It gonna
burn clear to the ground."

Sarah hurried to put her arms around Minta and hug her
tight. "I'm just Sarah now, remember? The house doesn'
matter. You saved the Row, the women and children, and
you saved me. I'll never forget that." She turned and lifted
Bessie into her arms. "And you, too, Bessie," she said, giv
ing her a big hug. "You were such a brave girl."

But Bessie hung her head. "I be bad, Mama."

Minta frowned. "Bad?"

"I got scared, Mama. I gonna go find you."

Minta looked into Sarah's face, her eyes wide with fear
Then she frowned at Bessie. "I tol' you not to leave this
cabin, chil'. Not for nothing."

"I know, Mama." A tear stood in Bessie's eye, and her
bottom lip quivered. "I scared. But I didn't go." Bessie's
little brightened. "Auntie help me. We say the words."

"Words?" Minta repeated.

"Yeah, Mama. The Bible words. 'The LORD is my shep
herd.' We said 'em over and over. And I stayed. Like you
said, Mama."

"Thank the Lord Jesus," Minta said. She looked at Sarah
And then they sank to their knees, all three of them, an
gave thanks to God.

twenty-two

Mid-April 1865

"I can't believe it's over," Willie said, slumping wearily in the saddle. "The war's really over."

"Yes," Calvin said, his voice hoarse with exhaustion. They'd been riding for days, catching an hour's sleep here, a few minutes' rest there, never able to relax, never really feeling safe, always with information that needed to be somewhere else. "It's over and we can go home."

"Miss Sarah's going to be happy to see us. Minta, too." Willie grinned. "And I want to see that Bessie. Bet she's grown a lot."

"Yes," Calvin said, trying to sound cheerful. Time enough for Willie to grieve when he learned who was lost. There hadn't been any word from Sarah for so long. It'd been months since he'd had a letter. Hiram was all right; he knew that much. Hiram had been in the hospital in Philadelphia when they'd passed through there a week or so ago. But soon he'd be on his way home. If he had a home to go to. That was the thing that bothered Calvin. What would they find when they reached Hawthorne Hill? The thought ate at his heart and soul. Was Sarah still alive? There'd been so much fighting. So many Yankee raids in and around the plantation area. Anything could have happened to her. Anything at all.

So many good men had died. He'd been with some of

them, seen them pass on. So many good women had been
hurt, lost their loved ones, been killed themselves. Why
should he and his loved ones fare any better? God might
have promised to be with His people, but He hadn'
promised to spare them the pain of loss.

Calvin pushed the horse a little harder. He had to ge
there. He had to know the worst.

Shortly before dawn they reached Hawthorne Hill
Willie had long ago stopped asking why they didn't res
and go on again in the morning. He just trailed along
silently, slumped down, half asleep.

As they turned up the lane between the great oaks, the
moon came out from behind the clouds, and Calvin cried
out in horror. "*No!* Please, God, no!"

Willie jerked awake. "What? What's wrong?"

"It's gone! Willie, the Big House is gone!" And he se
spurs to his stallion and galloped up the hill.

Hampered by a slower horse, Willie followed. By the
time he reached the top of the hill, Calvin was on his
knees, sobbing in the ashes. "She's gone," he cried. "My
Sarah's gone."

"Massa! Massa!" Willie was tugging at his jacket. Calvin
could feel that, but it didn't matter. He'd told the boy to
stop calling him Massa, but that didn't matter either
Nothing mattered now. His feelings of foreboding had
been true. Sarah was gone. He wanted to lie down in the
ashes himself and die. The war being over meant nothing
now. Without Sarah—

"Massa," Willie was saying, still tugging at his sleeve
"You got to get up. Miss Sarah around here somewhere
Minta take care of her. I know it."

Hope crept into Calvin's heart, the faintest glimmer, bu

enough to make him raise his head. "But the Big House—"

"Massa," Willie said, trying to shake him and pull him up at the same time. "People don't stay in no house when t burning down."

"But if the soldiers got her—" Thinking about that was almost worse than thinking that she was dead.

"Massa," Willie insisted. "Get up now. We got to find Minta and see what happened. That's what we gotta do."

Slowly Calvin pushed himself to his feet. He was so weary, with a weariness that no amount of sleep could ease. These past weeks his dreams had been haunted by the things he'd seen, the burned shells of houses that had once been homes, the blood, the mangled bodies, the grieving women. His fear for Sarah had grown and grown. But he had been under orders—he couldn't leave to go to her. He couldn't protect her from any of it. And now he had the awful feeling that it was too late, that she was gone.

But the war was over. Finally the fighting and killing could stop. And Willie wanted to see his sister, if she was here. Willie half-pushed, half-pulled him down the path toward Slave Row. Calvin let him, fear fighting with hope in his heart.

"Look, Massa," Willie cried as they turned the corner. "Minta's cabin's still there! They all still there. See!"

"I see." The cabins stood, solid blocks of darkness in the predawn light. He mustn't hope. It would hurt too much to hope and be wrong. But he started to run anyway, pushing his exhausted body to the limit. He had to know for sure. Whatever it was—he had to know.

Willie was right beside him. "Minta," he yelled. "Minta, wake up! We home!"

They burst through the door into the darkened cabin and Calvin's legs refused to take another step. He fell to his knees on the earthen floor, gasping for breath. *Please God, let her be here.*

Three shadowy figures detached themselves from the cornhusk mattress. He squinted through the darkness, hoping, praying.

"Willie? Is Calvin with you?"

"Sarah?" he breathed, hardly able to believe his ears. "Oh, thank You, God—Sarah."

And then she was running to him, throwing herself at him so hard that she knocked him flat on the packed earth floor. He didn't care. She was there, actually there, alive and in his arms, covering his face with kisses. He didn't care about anything but holding her close, while Willie chanted, "I told you, Massa! I told you! Minta take care of Miss Sarah."

"She did, too," Sarah said, easing out of his arms and helping him sit up. He gazed at her sweet face, lit now by faint moonlight, the face he'd never thought to see again in this life. "Minta and the other women convinced the Yankees that they wanted to burn the Big House," Sarah said. "And Bessie—" She looked over to where the little girl had wrapped herself around Willie's leg and was hanging on for dear life. "Bessie pretended to be sick and kept them from burning down the Row."

"And Auntie," Bessie piped up. "Auntie and me say the Bible words. So's I didn't get scared and run out, like Mama tol' me not to."

"Praise God," Calvin breathed. He got to his feet and pulled Sarah into his arms again. He never wanted to let go of her. "I thought— When I saw the Big House was nothing

ut ashes, I thought—God help me, Sarah, I lost my faith. I
hought you were gone."

"God kept us safe," Sarah said. "He brought us all
hrough."

"All but my Hiram," Minta said, her voice a mere whis-
er. "If only—"

"Hiram's all right," Calvin said, turning to her. "I'm sorry,
Minta. I should have told you sooner. He was in the hospital
n Philadelphia when we passed through there about a week
go. He was getting better. I'm sure he'll be heading home
oon."

"Praise the Lord Jesus," Minta cried, grabbing up Bessie
nd whirling her around and around the little cabin in a
oyful dance. "Your daddy's a-comin' home! Your daddy's
-comin' home!"

"Oh, Calvin," Sarah said, wrapping her arms around him
ightly. "I'm so glad you're safe. I was so worried, so
fraid—"

Willie grinned at them. "You got to trust in the Lord," he
aid.

Calvin chuckled. "The boy's right." He straightened. "We
nustn't forget that—to trust in God—now that we're mak-
ng a new beginning."

"Yes," Sarah said, sliding an arm around his waist. "I've
een thinking what to do. Now that the war's over I want
o divide the plantation so that everyone has a share."

"We'll rebuild the Big House and—"

"No," she said, putting her fingers over his lips. "That
ife is over. We'll build a small house, next door to Hiram
nd Minta's. We'll live like the others."

"Yes," he said, smiling at her. "But we're going to need
ne extra plot of ground."

"But, Calvin," she protested, "I don't want any more than the others."

His beautiful, good Sarah. He laughed. And to think that moments ago he'd thought never to laugh again.

"It isn't for us," he said. "It's for Willie. To build his school on. He's going to teach his people to read."

"Kin he teach me?" Minta asked.

"Of course," Calvin said. "He'll teach anyone who wants to learn."

"Me!" Bessie cried, pulling on Willie's shirt. "Me want to learn!"

"We'll start today," Willie said, lifting her in his arms. "Look, Bessie, the sun's coming up."

Calvin and Sarah turned to the window, where the first rays of the morning sun were lighting the earth.

"Yes," Sarah said. "The sun is coming up on our new life."

"A life we'll dedicate to God," Calvin said. "To God who brought us through this awful time."

"Amen," they said, all of them bowing their heads. "Amen."

A Letter To Our Readers

Dear Reader:

In order that we might better contribute to your reading enjoyment, we would appreciate your taking a few minutes to respond to the following questions. We welcome your comments and read each form and letter we receive. When completed, please return to the following:

Rebecca Germany, Fiction Editor
Heartsong Presents
PO Box 719
Uhrichsville, Ohio 44683

1. Did you enjoy reading *Neither Bond Nor Free?*
   - ☐ Very much. I would like to see more books
     by this author!
   - ☐ Moderately
     I would have enjoyed it more if _____

   _____

   _____

2. Are you a member of **Heartsong Presents**? Yes ☐ No ☐
   If no, where did you purchase this book?_____

   _____

3. How would you rate, on a scale from 1 (poor) to 5 (superior),
   the cover design?_____

4. On a scale from 1 (poor) to 10 (superior), please rate the
   following elements.

   _____ Heroine   _____ Plot

   _____ Hero   _____ Inspirational theme

   _____ Setting   _____ Secondary characters

5. These characters were special because _____

_____

_____

6. How has this book inspired your life? _____

_____

_____

7. What settings would you like to see covered in future **Heartsong Presents** books? _____

_____

_____

8. What are some inspirational themes you would like to see treated in future books? _____

_____

_____

9. Would you be interested in reading other **Heartsong Presents** titles?   Yes ❑   No ❑

10. Please check your age range:
    ❑ Under 18   ❑ 18-24   ❑ 25-34
    ❑ 35-45   ❑ 46-55   ❑ Over 55

11. How many hours per week do you read? _____

Name _____

Occupation _____

Address _____

City _____ State _____ Zip _____

Experience a family

saga that begins in 1860 when the painting of a homestead is first given to a young bride who leaves her beloved home of Laurelwood. Then follow the painting through a legacy of love that touches down in the years 1890, 1969, and finally today. Authors Sally Laity, Andrea Boeshaar, Yvonne Lehman, and DiAnn Mills have worked together to create a timeless treasure of four novellas in one collection.

paperback, 352 pages, 5 ³/₁₆" x 8"

❤ ❤ ❤ ❤ ❤ ❤ ❤ ❤ ❤ ❤ ❤ ❤ ❤ ❤ ❤ ❤ ❤ ❤ ❤ ❤

❤ ❤ ❤ ❤ ❤ ❤ ❤ ❤ ❤ ❤ ❤ ❤ ❤ ❤ ❤ ❤ ❤ ❤ ❤ ❤

····Hearts♥ng····

Any 12 *Heartsong* Presents titles for only $26.95 *

HISTORICAL ROMANCE IS CHEAPER BY THE DOZEN!
Buy any assortment of twelve *Heartsong Presents* titles and save 25% off of the already discounted price of $2.95 each!

*plus $1.00 shipping and handling per order and sales tax where applicable.

HEARTSONG PRESENTS TITLES AVAILABLE NOW:

(If ordering from this page, please remember to include it with the order form.)

·······Presents·······

Heartsong Presents
Love Stories
Are Rated G!

That's for godly, gratifying, and of course, great! If you love
thrilling love story, but don't appreciate the sordidness of son
popular paperback romances, **Heartsong Presents** is for you.
fact, **Heartsong Presents** is the *only inspirational romance bo*
club featuring love stories where Christian faith is the prima
ingredient in a marriage relationship.

Sign up today to receive your first set of four, never befo
published Christian romances. Send no money now; you w
receive a bill with the first shipment. You may cancel at any ti
without obligation, and if you aren't completely satisfied w
any selection, you may return the books for an immediate refun

Imagine. . .four new romances every four weeks—two h
torical, two contemporary—with men and women like you w
long to meet the one God has chosen as the love of their live
.all for the low price of $9.97 postpaid.

To join, simply complete the coupon below and mail to
address provided. **Heartsong Presents** romances are rated G
another reason: They'll arrive *Godspeed!*